Curiosity got the best of her...

Grace opened her mailbox and removed the large brown envelope. Her name and address had been printed in neat block letters, but there was no return address. She studied it for a moment wondering who had sent it. It weighed next to nothing. What could it be?

Curiosity got the best of her and she pulled the strip to open the envelope. Peering inside she saw a silk ivory scarf.

"What in the world?" She pulled it out and a piece of paper fluttered to the ground. The scarf draped luxuriously across her arm. The silk shimmered in the morning sunlight. She ran her hand down the length, its simplistic beauty mesmerizing her. She loved the feel of silk. Her one vice was silk lingerie, though she kept that secret to herself.

Last night Tyler had kissed her goodnight after walking her to the door. Could this be a present from him? He said that her skin looked and felt like ivory silk. No matter how she fought against it, she was falling for Tyler. He made her feel beautiful, not outside, but inside where for so long she'd felt soiled.

Praise for Carol Ann Erhardt

HIT AND RUN, September 2006 from The Wild Rose Press

"Hit and Run is a captivating read. The connection between the two sisters is awesome. I felt it uncanny how they could practically feel the others' sensations. Ms. Erhardt takes a well-developed plot and weaves a stunning read that puts the reader in the center of the action. With refreshing characters and some mystery along the way, she pens a wonderful story that keeps the pages turning." *Cherokee ~ Reviewer for Coffee Time Romance*

Foxfire

by

Carol Ann Erhardt

Foxfire

Contact Information: info@thewildrosepress.com

Cover Art by *Tamra Westberry*

The Wild Rose Press
PO Box 706
Adams Basin, NY 14410-0706
Visit us at www.thewildrosepress.com

Publishing History
Crimson Rose Edition, January 2006
ISBN 1-60154-029-9

Published in the United States of America

Dedication

Thanks to Lee Duran for helping me during the entire writing process on this story. Thanks to my editor, Ally Robertson. Thank you to my "family" for reading the rough draft and giving me feedback, my husband for his support, and God for showing me the path.

Chapter One

"I'm sure you understand that given the circumstances we can't be married."

Connor's words hit Grace with the force of an invisible fist. The restaurant sounds grew louder with multiple conversations, a burst of laughter and the clink of silverware on fine china. All normal sounds in a normal world.

Connor lifted his crystal goblet as if to propose a toast to the termination of their engagement.

Beneath the artificial lights, the diamond on Grace's finger winked lewdly. She yanked it off and dropped it into Connor's glass of merlot, where it landed with a satisfactory clink.

"You hypocritical bastard."

He slammed the goblet on the table, sending forth a shower of wine. With an oath, he mopped at the spots of red on his otherwise pristine, and very expensive, designer shirt.

"Damn it, Grace, look what you've done."

"*I* haven't done anything." Her voice rose. "What happened to innocent until proven guilty? Who made you judge and juror?" More angry words sat on the tip of her tongue, but she squelched them. She slammed her hands on the table and leaned into his face. "You're off the hook, Counselor." Grace's voice turned the heads of the couple seated at the table next to them.

Connor gazed over the glasses resting on his nose. His eyes, which once heated her blood, now froze her with a blast of contempt.

"For God's sake, keep your voice down."

Grace pushed her chair back and walked away, defying the bulls-eye she felt between her shoulder

1

blades. The press loved Connor Thomas, prosecuting attorney and aspiring senator. At any moment she expected an eager reporter to jump out and blind her with flashbulbs. She maneuvered her way through the throng of waiting customers, pushed open the doors of the restaurant and burst into the warm Tennessee night.

People passed, some giving her a quick glance, others too wrapped in their own world to notice. Her temples throbbed, amplifying the pain, the resentment, and the anger. The parking garage loomed ahead—only a short block away. She stepped off the curb and her foot landed at an awkward slant, her ankle twisting painfully. With a muffled gasp, she lurched forward. She might have fallen had a male passerby not reached out to steady her.

"Are you all right?"

She nodded through her tears.

The woman beside him gazed at her with concern.

"I'm fine," Grace insisted in a shaky voice. "Really."

She continued on, ignoring the agony twisting through her body like a buzz saw. The hollow sound of her footsteps followed her to the parking garage, and she jabbed the elevator button. The ancient mechanism clunked and clanged, but climbed higher. She waited until it stopped and punched it again but the elevator didn't move.

With a curse, she entered the dark fetid stairwell. Pulling her shoulders toward her chest to avoid brushing the stained walls, she surged up the stairs gagging at the vile odor of urine-soaked concrete.

She plunged through the door and took a breath. Behind the elevator, metal scraped on concrete. She held her breath and listened, but heard no further noise. She placed her keys between her fingers and hurried toward her car. The click-click of her footsteps picked up pace, battling the thud-thud of her heartbeat. She reached her car and fumbled with the lock. Finally, she slid beneath the steering wheel.

The car's interior light winked out, leaving her and

her tumbling thoughts in semi-darkness. How had Connor learned her secret? He had the means to check into her background, but why had he waited until now? They'd worked together for a year, been engaged for six months, and never once had he seemed interested in her past. Evidently, she'd been mistaken.

Once again, she heard the sound of metal grating across the floor. For endless seconds she held her breath, listening to her own racing heartbeat.

With palsied fingers, she turned the key and the motor roared to life. She glanced through the rear window and inched her car out of the narrow parking space. Her headlight beams illuminated a man standing next to the elevator. Their eyes made contact, and with a sense of unease, she pressed the accelerator and sped toward the exit.

She thought the man was most likely one of the city's homeless, of which there were many. Some lived on the streets because they had lost jobs and homes, while others had drifted there due to addictions. Once, had she not been strong enough to fight, she might have become one of the faceless forgotten souls.

She paid her parking fee and merged onto the busy street, longing to get home where she could lick her wounds in private, but every traffic light conspired against her.

"Come on," she urged the red beacon holding her prisoner. She swiped at an angry tear running down her cheek. A haunting country tune wafted from the speakers, lamenting a broken heart and lost dreams.

"Damn." With the push of a button she stifled the singer's pain.

****

Twenty minutes later, Grace Wilkins entered the sanctuary of home.

"Tiff, here girl. Where are you?" She turned on the lamp, flooding the living room with light, but there was no sign of her canine friend.

3

Grace tossed her purse on the sofa, kicked off her shoes, and padded to the kitchen. The humiliation she'd swallowed had formed into a lead cannonball in her stomach. She rummaged through the refrigerator and pulled out a partial bottle of wine. She poured herself a glass and carried it to the bedroom, hoping it would help kill the parasites of anger and hurt chewing her from inside out. She stepped out of her slacks and quickly removed her other clothes, assessing her body in the mirror. She frowned. Her hips were fuller than fashionably acceptable in today's world, especially for someone of her short stature. Her breasts, while not Playboy material, weren't too bad. Her best feature was her naturally curly red hair. She looked normal on the outside, no visible scars. The scars were inside where she kept them hidden from the rest of the world. Connor had inflicted another one tonight.

She wrapped herself in her worn terrycloth robe, then sank onto the mattress and stared into the mirror at her own haunted gaze. Silently, she asked the image if it would have been so wrong for her to marry, have a decent home, maybe one or two kids? She'd been so close to fulfilling her dreams. If only—

The pet door rattled and Tiffany's claws scrabbled across the kitchen floor. The black and white collie-lab bounded through the bedroom door, waving her tail like a banner.

The dog gave a short bark. Ninety pounds of animal leaned against Grace's leg.

"Where've you been?" Grace sat the wine on the nightstand and ruffled the dog's fur with both hands. Tiffany gazed at her with total adoration, freeing the tears Grace could no longer stifle. They streamed down her cheeks and she slipped to the floor, throwing her arms around the dog's neck. Grace burrowed her face in the soft black fur and her shoulders heaved. Deep coughing sobs erupted from the depth of her scarred soul.

Tiffany squirmed closer and licked at Grace's damp

cheeks. Suddenly the dog stilled and her ears perked. At a knock on the door, she hurtled away.

Grace grabbed a tissue and blew her nose. Only one person would come calling this time of night—Brad, her next-door neighbor and the closest thing to a grandfather she'd ever had. Tonight she wasn't eager for his company. She didn't want him to see her broken spirit. Not even if he could *almost* make her believe she deserved more out of life.

Tiffany whined at the front door, nose to the crack.

Grace flicked on the porch light and opened the door without looking through the peephole.

Tiffany nosed the wooden screen door, squeezed through, and jumped to rest her front paws against the chest of a man Grace had never seen before. Grace stepped outside, letting the screen door close behind her.

The dog's tail wagged so fast a breeze stirred the robe Grace clutched tightly against her chest. She held it together with one hand and reached blindly with the other for the belt. Finally she secured the two ends in a semi-knot.

"Down, Tiff," she ordered.

Her visitor laughed, a deep warm from-the-toes burst of mirth. He rubbed the dog's neck and gently sent her back to all fours.

"It's all right. We're old friends."

Tiffany plopped at his feet and stared up at Grace with a panting smile.

The man's gaze fell to Grace's bare feet, and then lifted slowly, heating her blood inch by inch.

"Sorry if I've caught you at a bad time." Emerald eyes locked on hers, belying his apology. "Tyler Sandford." He held his hand out. Laugh lines added character to his handsome face. "I'm your neighborhood veterinarian. I bought the house through that stand of trees." He nodded to his left.

He *had* caught her at a bad time. She jutted out her chin, daring him to acknowledge her puffy eyes and red nose. She let go of her robe and gripped his hand firmly. "Grace Wilkins."

Why hadn't she checked before opening the door? What must he think of the half-naked, sniffling, weak-assed woman before him? And why did she care? Somewhere deep inside, hurt knocked against Grace's ribs. She pulled her hand out of his warm grip, and adjusted the robe to protect her cleavage. Grace nodded at her dog, who acted as if she'd found a new best friend. "And this is Tiffany."

His emerald eyes held her gaze, pulling her in, magnetizing her. "You have a beautiful name, Grace."

God, what kind of line was he dealing? She hated her name. She didn't even have a middle name since her mother hadn't given her only daughter one. She was Grace Wilkins. Period. No middle name. No middle initial. One man had dubbed her Gracie Jo. She suppressed a shudder.

Tyler's heated glance threatened to melt her armor, but she stood strong against the assault. She'd met his kind many times. His dark hair and equally dark lashes set off his chiseled face. He was handsome, flirtatious and most likely unfaithful.

She eased back toward the door. "Did you stop by to borrow a cup of sugar?"

Obviously unfazed by her saccharine barb, he knelt beside the dog. "Your dog and I met on the path in the woods." His chin rose to avoid Tiffany's tongue. "I followed her here, noticed your lights on, and decided to introduce myself."

Grace stared. Both of his knees shone through the gaping holes in his threadbare, tattered jeans. Dirty tennis shoes peeked from beneath the ragged cuffs. Though they were in the foothills of the Smoky Mountains where people didn't exactly dress for success, his attire didn't fit her image of a veterinarian.

Grace snapped her fingers signaling Tiffany, but the dog remained frozen to Tyler's side.

His dark smoldering gaze swept down Grace's bare legs, and a smile teased the corners of his mouth. Slowly he rose to his full height to tower over her.

If he thought she'd succumb to his not-so-charming come-on, he'd be disappointed. He didn't know the real woman behind the tear-ravaged face. "So we've met now." Grace placed her hand on the gap of the robe and pressed her knees together. "As you can see, I'm not exactly dressed for company."

His gaze caressed her again, pausing briefly where her hand clutched the robe above her racing heart.

"Looks good to me."

When he leaned closer as if to share a secret, she caught and held her breath. "You have something on your face." His fingers touched her cheek and came away holding a piece of tissue. "Got it."

The tissue floated to the wooden floor.

"I apologize for dropping by so late. I just wanted to put in a plug for business."

He was so close, the crisp citrus scent of his cologne stroked her senses. With shocking awareness, she watched his nostrils flare. She took a step backward, regaining her space. Beneath the thin robe, goose bumps danced on her body. The phenomenon had nothing to do with the temperature and everything to do with this unwelcome visitor standing on her porch.

She put her hand on the screen door and began to pull it open.

"I'll bring Tiffany by for her yearly shots. Maybe in six months or so."

"You don't have to wait that long." His lashes kissed his cheekbone in a lazy wink. "Come down any time. I'll give you a tour." He ran his hand down Tiffany's back and as Grace watched, she felt her own body quiver just like the dog's.

"I have to go." The door squeaked on its hinges as Grace backed into the open doorway.

The slight upward curve to her visitor's lips and the

gleam in his eyes told her everything. He knew what she was feeling. She was an idiot. Earlier tonight another man had spurned her. So much for new beginnings. She was what she was.

She opened the door and snapped her fingers. "Come, Tiff."

Tiffany whacked her tail against the porch floor.

Tyler lifted his shoulders in a shrug toward his not-so-innocent smile and nudged the dog with his foot.

Tiffany lumbered to her feet and walked into the house.

"See you around." Tyler nodded in farewell.

"Good night."

"Yes, it is," he said. A wicked grin lifted his lips and traveled up his face, igniting his unusually deep green eyes. He winked, pivoted, and strode off toward the woods.

Grace stared through the screen until the darkness and trees swallowed his outline, then she closed and locked the door.

"Traitor. I suppose you still expect me to feed you."

Tiffany whined, her eyes remorseful.

"You like him, huh?"

A tail waved in response.

"Did you notice his eyes? I've never seen eyes that color before. I suppose he wears contacts."

Grace dipped the plastic dish in the dog food bag. "Doesn't matter if the color's real or not, he's still sexy."

Tiffany whuffed softly.

Grace placed the bowl on the floor and headed for the shower. She spied the glass of wine she'd poured earlier and dumped it down the sink. She'd lost the urge to drink away her pain. Her new neighbor might be an outrageous flirt, but he'd been a soothing balm to her bruised ego.

After her shower, she slipped into a silk and lace nightgown, one of her vices, and snuggled beneath the cool sheets. Tiffany stretched across the foot of the bed.

Grace closed her eyes. Soon her new neighbor's face

formed into a sensual dream-like vision. She knew instinctively there'd be no holding back with a man like him. Everything would be spontaneous, exciting, and passionate. She lost herself in the fantasy, in a heated kiss that seared her soul. She gazed into deep emerald fire that sparked like the gem.

Suddenly the image began to shift and the green eyes turned to steely gray hiding behind plastic lenses. The heat of passion turned to fetid flames of viscous evil. Fingers dug into her shoulders. Connor's voice rasped, "The media would have a hey-day if they learned my future wife used to be a prostitute." His polished attorney smile, all white dazzling teeth, flashed behind her eyes. The scene in the restaurant kept repeating over and over, like a movie in perpetual play.

Grace rolled over and punched the pillow. She hadn't been a prostitute.

Well, not exactly.

****

Tyler climbed the back stairs of the clinic, which led to his apartment above. He flicked on the lights and took off his jacket and shoulder holster. The gun clunked against the heavy wooden kitchen table. He reached for his cell phone and dialed his boss.

"I made contact tonight," Tyler informed Jake when he answered.

"Good. Before you tell me, listen up. We've been following a lead in South America. If it pans out, I'll have a picture for you in a few days."

"What about Ted Powell?"

"Nada."

"So maybe Max isn't here at all. I've been scouting the area every day, but so far, everything seems normal."

"Tell me about your contact with Grace Wilkins."

What could he tell him? That she had curves reminiscent of the starlets of the 50's, nicely rounded hips that a man's hands could grip, or that her million dollar legs should be insured? Or should he confess that looking into her deep blue eyes he glimpsed a vulnerability hidden behind her tough façade? Her picture hadn't fully prepared him for the flesh and blood woman.

"Not much to tell," he finally said. "I caught her at a bad time, introduced myself and that's about it." Except that he had always been a sucker for tears. Some women couldn't hide the evidence. Grace was one of them. She had the light complexion and freckles that led him to believe her red riotous curls didn't come from a bottle.

"An introduction is a start, I guess," Jake conceded. "Just do your best to keep an eye on her. I've no doubt Max will surface, and I don't want him to strike when we're not looking and get away. She's our best lead right now. We'll keep looking for Ted Powell. If anything comes up, I'll call you."

Tyler ran a hand through his hair. "All right. I'm going to maintain my cover as long as possible."

"How are you doing with the clinic?"

"I'm running an ad this weekend. Everything's coming along."

"I hope for your sake it works out. I support your decision, bro. You know that."

"I know and I appreciate it."

Tyler dropped into the chair and lifted his feet to the coffee table. "Max will surface sooner or later. We'll get him Jake. For Natalie."

There was a brief silence before Jake responded.

"Yeah, for Natalie. Keep in touch."

The phone cut off and Tyler tossed it to the table.

For Natalie, yeah right. If he'd wanted to do something for Natalie, maybe he should have quit his job like she'd begged him to do. Maybe if he had, she'd still be alive...and so would the child she carried inside her.

"One last assignment, Natalie," he said to the empty room. "I promise this time. I'll quit as soon as I bury the sonofabitch that took you from me."

Tyler couldn't bring back his wife or their baby, and he'd live with that loss the rest of his life, but he had an

10

opportunity to avenge their deaths. He might spend the rest of his life feeling guilty, but he'd bring Max Clayton down, even if it meant using Grace Wilkins to do it.

Chapter Two

The next morning, Grace stared across the horizon at the haze hanging over the distant mountain range. Dew clung to the bushes lining the driveway, glittering in the few rays of sun breaking through the trees surrounding her cabin home. The scene in the restaurant last night seemed a faraway memory.

Tiffany padded into the kitchen and bumped her head against Grace's leg. "Okay, Tiff. I know it's time for work, but I'm not going."

The dog tilted her head questioningly.

"I quit. Connor and I broke up." She held her hand in front of the dog's nose. "See, no ring. I don't work for him any more."

She ran her fingers through the dog's soft fur. "Don't worry, I'll find a job to keep you in doggie biscuits."

Tiffany whined.

"It's okay, girl." She cradled the dog's head in her palms and stared into chocolate brown eyes that gazed at her with uncanny understanding. "Everything will be fine. I'm a survivor. I always land on my feet."

Tiffany thumped her tail against the floor.

The telephone rang, disturbing their camaraderie.

Grace glared at the offending apparatus, but it continued to ring. She snatched the receiver off the hook, and just as she'd expected, Connor's voice grated through the line.

"Why the hell aren't you at work?"

"I quit."

"We have to talk."

"I think you said it all last night, Connor."

"You can't quit. Not without giving notice."

12

"I can. I just did."

He heaved an angry sounding breath. "I don't want to broadcast our broken engagement until we find a way to do it without raising questions."

"What *you* want doesn't matter. Not any longer."

"Damn it, Grace. What do you expect from me?"

"Not a damn thing."

"I think you should come back to work, at least for a while. If we do this right, the press will—"

She slammed the phone down. His arrogant, demanding tone took the pain that had begun to fester again and stuffed it down deep inside. So he was worried, huh? Well, Mr. Hot Shot attorney had made a big mistake. The Knoxville Sentinel might hurt his career, but it couldn't hurt her. Politics was his game, not hers.

Someone whistled and Tiffany raced out the pet door. Brad on his morning stroll no doubt. The thought of seeing her friend drove her out the door and onto the path between their houses. She caught up with Brad and Tiffany a few seconds later. When he spied her, Brad's lined and weathered face lit with happy surprise. Then concern drove the smile away.

"Why aren't you at work? Are you sick?"

Grace shook her head and her shield crumbled as she fell into Brad's arms. His warm broad palm patted her back. Her cheek pressed against his shoulder. She inhaled the comforting outdoorsy scent of his after-shave, feeling more like a small child than a twenty-four year old woman.

Brad was her surrogate grandfather. He'd nurtured their relationship since the day she moved next door to him. Tiffany had been his first Christmas present to her, a small fluffy black and white, clumsy-footed ball of fur.

"What's wrong, honey?" he asked.

"Oh, Brad, everything. My whole life is wrong."

He turned her toward his house. "Come on. You can tell me all about it over a bowl of home-made ice cream."

"It's still morning," Grace sniffled.

"Yeah? So what?"

Grace wiped her nose. "Strawberry with lots of chocolate syrup?"

"What else?" He chuckled and ruffled the fur on Tiffany's head. "Come on, girl."

In Brad's kitchen, Grace pulled the bottle of chocolate from the refrigerator while Brad scooped the ice cream. She squeezed chocolate syrup into the bowl he pushed in front of her and licked the sticky sweet residue from her fingers.

Sun rays beamed brightly through the window above the sink. Tiffany grunted as she lowered her body onto the tiled floor. Grace loved the blue and white gingham curtains, which lifted softly in the light breeze blowing through the open window. This room had been a haven where she and Brad shared many hours discussing events in their lives. He had built the butcher block table himself, though the ladder back chairs were not his handiwork. Light blue rugs in front of the sink and refrigerator matched the blue shade in the curtains, and warmed the otherwise rustic room. Like Grace's house, the walls were log and mortar, lending an authenticity to the cabin architecture. Brad's kitchen gave credence to the phrase, "the kitchen is the heart of the home."

He sat across from her and met her gaze. "So what's going on? What's with the tears? You never cry."

Grace held out her hand and wiggled her bare left fingers. "Connor called off the engagement last night."

His head bowed. Thinning strands of still-dark hair allowed glimpses of his scalp. He lifted her hand and ran his gnarled fingers over the place where the ring used to be. Then he looked at her, his kind blue eyes full of understanding.

"He wasn't good enough for you, honey."

Grace pulled her hand away.

"That's not true, Brad. It's the other way around. I wasn't good enough. I'm not good enough for any man. That's the problem." She stuffed a huge bite of ice cream in her mouth. Pain shot across her forehead—instant brain freeze.

"Want to tell me what happened?" Brad's gentle voice soothed her.

Grace shook her head.

Brad leaned back in his chair. "I can guess. Connor found out about your past?"

"Yeah."

"Honey, do you think things would have been different if he'd found out *after* you got married?"

She sniffed and blew her nose on a paper towel.

"Well, do you?" he persisted.

"No," she admitted. "I'm stupid for thinking it could work."

"Only marriages based on love work, honey."

"You're a fine one to talk. Don't tell me that's why you haven't popped the question to Harri. I know you—"

"Uh-uh." Brad moved his finger back and forth in front of her face. "This conversation is about you, not me."

Grace silenced her retort with another bite of ice cream. Brad was right. He tried to warn her when she plunged headlong into the doomed relationship. She planned to tell Connor the truth about her past, but the timing had never seemed right.

She sighed and laid her spoon on the table. "I quit my job. I just couldn't face working at the D.A.'s office where I'd see him every day."

Brad nodded. "Makes sense. You'll find another job. And, there are other fish in the sea, as Harri always tells me."

"Not for me. I'm never going to fall in love."

"That's something you have no control over. When the real thing comes along, you'll be caught up so quick you won't know what hit you. Mark my words, you'll see."

"No man will ever want me."

"You're wrong." He tapped her hand. "You're a beautiful, strong woman, inside and out. Any man would be fortunate to have you."

She concentrated on her bowl of ice cream. One thing she'd learned well. Arguing with Brad was a losing proposition. The day after she moved in, he'd knocked on her door with a frozen container of homemade ice cream. Their friendship had flourished and before long she felt safe in telling him about her troubled childhood. She shared the nightmare of growing up with a mother who would snuggle her one minute and rage at her the next. Brad listened without judgment when she confessed the truth about her past. She told herself it was to protect him if her enemies should find her. The truth was she needed someone to accept her and love her no matter how stained her life had been.

Brad's heart was bigger than anyone's she'd ever known. He hadn't blinked an eye. Just listened. When she finished, he hugged her, told her he thought she was brave and admirable. Then he offered to make dinner as if she'd just confessed she was a super-star.

His voice broke into her thoughts. "You think too much, honey."

She reached across the table and squeezed his hand. "Do you know how much I love you, Brad?"

He dipped his head like a bashful boy and muttered, "Yeah, I know."

They finished eating in a comfortable silence. Grace realized the rock that had been sitting on top of her heart had disappeared. What would she do without Brad? Her life would be empty. Lonely. No ice cream to soothe her soul. Why had she shed tears over a man she didn't love? Would she feel empty or lonely without Connor? Honestly, no. A life without Connor wouldn't be the same as a life without Brad. She longed to be part of a family, but maybe her vision of that didn't exist. The whole scenario of a house in the suburbs, children playing in the yard, a man greeting her with a kiss, complimenting her on the delicious smell of dinner simmering on the stove—it was all an illusion. Connor could never be that kind of man. But Brad would never let her down. Brad was her family.

As if reading her thoughts, he asked, "Do you have plans for dinner tonight?"

"No."

"Good. You do now. Harri's bringing dessert, some new recipe she found. I'm going to stir up a pot of my famous beef stew."

Grace grinned. "Count me in." She stood and reached for their empty bowls.

"Don't bother, hon, I'll clean up."

She brushed a kiss on his cheek and walked to the door. Holding it open, she called, "Come on, Tiff, time to go."

"Wear something nice," Brad said as the bowls clattered into the sink.

Grace looked at him questioningly. "What's so special about tonight?"

Brad shoved his hands in his pockets. His grin and twinkling eyes showed signs of the little boy he'd been some sixty-odd years ago, but he didn't offer an explanation.

What trick did her sneaky friend have up his sleeve? She flipped a wave. "See you later."

She hoped he wouldn't try to fix her up with Adam Shockley. Through a break in the trees, she looked up the hill at Adam's house. He was the one who sold her the cabin she called home. At one time, he probably owned the whole damn mountain. Over the years, he sold off most of the acreage. He was a bachelor and several years older than her. Sometimes Grace caught him looking at her in a way that made her skin crawl.

She hurried home and retrieved the newspaper. Job-hunting was critical. She wouldn't be able to afford her house payment, let alone buy groceries, if she didn't find another job soon. She opened the pages, spreading them flat and glanced at the front page.

Her breath imploded in a painful gasp. The headline screamed at her. Another woman had been found stabbed to death last night. The hairs raised on the back of

Grace's neck. Her heart thumped as she recalled the man she'd seen lurking in the parking garage—the same one where this latest victim had been discovered.

Oh, my God. Had Grace seen the killer?

Her temples began to pound. She took the aspirin bottle from the medicine cabinet and shook two into her hand. Just because she had seen something, a shadow no less, didn't mean she'd seen a killer. Lots of homeless people found shelter in the downtown garages at night.

She popped the aspirin in her mouth and rinsed them down with tepid water. Setting the glass on the counter, she wiped her mouth and stared through the window at the changing landscape. The white of the mountain laurel contrasted with deeper green pine trees creating a breathtaking forefront to the distant mountains. Spring was her favorite time of year, a time for new beginnings.

She was making a new beginning. Another chapter of her life had ended. Time to look forward, not backward. Forget about the murders. They had nothing to do with her.

Brad came into view, walking-stick in hand, plodding along the path. His familiar three-legged gait brought a smile to her lips. He was probably heading down to the new animal clinic. Brad kept tabs on what happened in the community, though he insisted he wasn't as bad as Adam Shockley. Adam personally welcomed each new Foxfire resident, and rumor had it that if you didn't pass his inspection, you'd be an outcast.

The new vet wouldn't have a problem getting along with the neighbors. He had an open personality, and if he flirted with the ladies like he had with Grace...well, he'd soon have a string of what Grace called "foo-foo" dogs for patients.

Maybe she'd bake some brownies as a welcome gift. Not because she wanted to see him again, of course, just a friendly gesture. Besides, he liked Tiffany, who definitely wasn't a "foo-foo" dog. Look toward new beginnings. Forget about the Knoxville Knifer and the murders.

Grace forced her gaze away from the window and massaged the back of her neck, squeezing to loosen the tight muscles. She headed to the living room, where Tiffany lifted an eyelid and gave her a one-second stare from her spot in front of the fireplace. Grace eased down in the rocking chair, setting it in motion. The gentle rhythmic creaking of wood on wood, along with the aspirin, eased the pounding in her temples, but didn't stop her conscience.

She'd have to tell the police what she'd seen. Every lead counted. She shuddered. What had gone through the minds of the women who had been murdered so savagely with a sharp blade? Once Grace had to defend herself against a knife-wielding assailant, and she'd been nearly blinded with fear.

Another shudder racked her.

****

Tyler lifted his head and crawled out from under the leaking sink. The bell jangled again, alerting him that someone had entered. Wiping his hands on his jeans, he hurried downstairs into the clinic.

"Hey, Tyler," Brad greeted.

"Brad. You're a sight for sore eyes." Tyler shook the hand of the elder man, which was surprisingly strong despite his age. "I was just wrestling with a leaky pipe. Are you psychic?" Brad had been hanging around for weeks checking the progress of the clinic, so seeing him this morning wasn't a surprise.

Brad winced as he slipped his arms from the light flannel jacket, a sign that his arthritis was troubling him this morning.

"If you want a hand with that leak, I'll see what I can do."

Tyler had no doubt Brad could fix it, but he didn't want the old man down on the floor. "Nah, it can wait." He nodded to the left. "Check out the new scale they delivered this morning."

Tyler pushed open a door and waited for Brad to

follow. Once inside the examination room, Tyler planted his foot on a stainless steel scale.

"Top of the line. Can accurately weigh a two-hundred pound Saint Bernard."

"Doubt if there's many of them around this neck of the woods."

Tyler said, "You never know what might come through these doors. I'm going to open the clinic next week. I placed an ad in the Foxfire News to run this weekend."

"Better to put it in the Knoxville Sentinel. Not that many people in Foxfire, son."

"I need to start small since I can't hire an assistant for a while." He still hoped to entice his dad to join him. But he had to deal with finding a killer first. The first person he'd hire would be someone to run the office for him, keep the books and appointments straight, but even that would have to wait until he actually had some clients.

Brad nodded, his blue eyes sharp with approval. "You're a smart business man."

"Thanks." Brad's praise felt good. Since Tyler had left Ohio, he missed having daily conversations with his dad. Quickly, he tamped down a painful memory.

Brad asked, "Got plans for dinner tonight?"

"Cold cut sandwiches. If you want to join me, I'll throw together a salad to go with them," Tyler answered.

Brad's deep rumbling laugh filled the room. "I've got a better offer. Come to my house for beef stew and some exotic dessert Harri's throwing together."

Tyler grinned broadly and clapped Brad on the shoulder. "What time?"

"Make it around six. Come on, son, let's go fix that leak."

****

Dusk had nearly given way to the cloudless blanket of night when Grace arrived at Brad's for dinner. She knocked and opened the door.

"Brad?"

Tiffany preceded her inside and bounded toward a surprised Tyler. But he couldn't be more surprised than Grace. What was he doing here?

"Grace, honey, come on in." Brad hurried forward and put an arm possessively around her shoulders. He turned to look at Tyler. "Let me introduce you to—"

"Grace, what a pleasant surprise." Tyler's emerald eyes swept over Grace with a glint of male appreciation, making her glad she'd chosen to wear her favorite blue blouse and black dress slacks. Tyler took her hand, wrapping his fingers tightly around hers. Her pulse leaped.

Brad beamed. "I didn't know you two had met."

Grace shifted her eyes to meet Tyler's teasing grin, then quickly looked down at their clasped hands. She pulled hers free. "We, uh..." She took a step sideways, giving herself room to breathe. "Tyler dropped by last night."

Tyler placed his hand on Grace's shoulder, giving it a brief squeeze.

"Tiffany led me to Grace's door, and I took the opportunity to introduce myself and tell her about the clinic."

A tap on the door turned all their heads. "Yoo hoo, I'm here. Better late than never, I always say." Harri burst through the door, her bright orange hair dimmed only by the turquoise earrings bobbing on her lobes. She stopped abruptly when she caught sight of Tyler.

Grace hurried forward. "Here let me take that," she said relieving Harri of an oblong pan.

Brad slid Harri's cardinal red sweater off her shoulders. "Harri, meet Tyler Sandford, our community veterinarian. Tyler, Harriet Parton. Better known as Harri."

Tyler lifted Harri's hand to his lips. "Ms. Parton, it's an honor to finally meet you. Brad's mentioned you many times. Are you relation to the famous Dolly?"

Harri yanked her hand back as if burned. "A distant cousin of sorts." Her voice dropped an octave and her lips turned downward. She narrowed her golden brown eyes, made more prominent by the lavish application of lavender eye shadow. "What's the old geezer been saying about me?"

"Only good things, I assure you," Tyler responded.

Harri looked him over from head to toe. "You have an interesting aura. Lots of green."

Tyler's eyebrows lifted questioningly. "Green?"

"Suits your profession. I see some dark purple, too." She lifted the glasses hanging on a beaded chain and slipped them onto her nose. "Interesting," she murmured. She removed the glasses and let them dangle around her neck.

Brad slipped his arm across Harri's shoulders and squeezed. "Now, Harri, don't get started with that nonsense." He smiled apologetically at Tyler. "Harri thinks she's psychic."

"Bradley Johnson." Harri's hands fisted on her ample hips. "One of these days you'll be sorry for doubting my abilities."

"Right, darlin'. So what did you bring for dessert?"

Harri ignored him and squinted farsightedly at Tyler. Grace knew that look. She almost felt sorry for him. She could practically feel him squirm under that scrutinizing gaze.

"I'm not sure of you yet, young man. Something's not right. But you can call me Harri."

Grace felt like giggling. The teasing, flirtatious veterinarian had met his match. She wondered what he thought about Harri's outrageous outfit—a long flowing broomstick skirt in blended splashes of red, gold and black, topped with a lime green poet's blouse. Only Harri could deck herself out like a peacock and still command respect. Her happy spirit invaded the room and brought a glow of love to Brad's eyes.

He ladled their plates with steaming beef stew that

made Grace's mouth water. The smell of freshly baked sourdough rolls wafted from the covered basket in the center of the table. She took one and passed the basket to Tyler, who sat so close their arms brushed when he took it. He winked and she slipped her hands to her lap to hide her trembling fingers. Damn him. He knew exactly what effect he had on her.

Tiffany plopped loudly onto the floor and huffed a sigh.

Brad's stomach jumped in time with his laughter. "I'm not forgetting you, girl. You just have to wait until it cools."

The dog's tail whacked the floor as she looked at him expectantly.

"Where did you come from, Tyler?" Harri asked.

Tyler coughed and choked on a bite of roll.

Grace grinned wickedly and pounded him on the back.

He covered his mouth with his napkin and slanted her a glance.

She lifted her eyebrows and smiled innocently.

"Sorry," he said turning his gaze to Harri. "I was born and raised in Ohio."

"Why did you move to Tennessee?" Harri demanded.

"I love the mountains. When I was a kid, our family vacationed in the Gatlinburg area. I've always wanted to live here. When the opportunity arose, I couldn't resist."

"What opportunity?" Harri prodded.

Brad's silverware clattered against his plate. "Harri, don't be so nosy. If Tyler wants—"

"It's all right, Brad. I don't mind. I was in partnership with...another vet. Things didn't work out, and here I am."

Harri's earrings swayed hypnotically as she buttered her roll with a vengeance. "Young man, you went from page one to the end and skipped the entire middle of that story."

Tyler chewed, studying his plate as if searching for a

proper response.

Harri slapped her knife onto the table. "You must let me read your palm sometime."

"Yes, Tyler," Grace piped in, her voice laced with saccharin. "You should let Harri read your palm."

Harri flicked a glance at Grace's bare finger.

"Hmmph. *You* should have listened to me, girl."

It was Grace's turn to cough.

"You should see Tyler's clinic," Brad interjected. "He's got a scale big enough to weigh a bear."

For a moment a heavy silence rent the air in the wake of Brad's obvious attempt to change the subject.

"Not quite," Tyler said. "Let's hope none of my clients has a bear for a pet."

"He's opening next week," Brad said. "Ran an ad in the local paper."

Harri's eyes dilated, fixing on Grace for a few heart-stopping seconds, and then focused on Tyler. Her gaze wavered, settling somewhere between the two of them.

Tyler nodded and reached for another roll. "It'll be slow to start, but I'm hoping to expand through word of mouth. Once I get an established client base, I'll hire someone to run the office. Appointments, billing, that sort of thing."

Brad lifted his fork and pointed at Grace. "Our Grace is looking for a job. Why not hire her?"

Grace felt her face flush. She wrapped her fingers around her glass to keep from throttling Brad. What in the world was he doing? First inviting this stranger to dinner in a not-too-subtle matchmaking ploy, then letting him know she was unemployed. Surrogate grandfather or not, he'd stepped over the line.

Brad cleared his throat and shoved away from the table. "I forgot about Tiffany." He placed a bowl in front of the dog and then washed his hands noisily. The running water and Tiffany's snapping jaws were the only sounds to be heard.

Tyler looked at Grace. "You have any experience with

computers?"

"Yes, but I'm not...that is, I just quit my job. I haven't thought a lot about what I'm going to do next."

Brad began to clear the table. "What's the mystery dessert, Harri?"

"Zodiac surprise," she responded quickly.

Anxiety and mirth brought a burst of laughter from Grace. Brad's deep booming guffaw joined in, followed by Tyler's more reserved chuckle.

Harri's face lit as if a candle glowed within. Dimples marked her chipmunk cheeks. "It's vanilla cake made with coconut rum. You'll love it, I swear."

Brad pressed a kiss on the top of Harri's head. "Darlin', I'm sure we will."

And they did, polishing off nearly the entire cake with much approbation for the cook. Grace insisted on washing dishes, shooing everyone else to the living room. She wanted time to herself away from Tyler's virile presence. Her mind wandered to how easily she responded to him and how she didn't miss Connor at all. How could she move so easily from one ruined relationship into feeling attracted to another man? Especially one she didn't know. He could be a pervert or maybe even the serial killer the cops were trying to find. What did she really know about him?

She placed the last dish in the drainer and reached for the dishtowel. Though she didn't hear a sound, she knew the moment Tyler entered the room.

He took the towel from her hands. "Allow me," he said.

Tyler stepped back and reached for an item in the draining rack.

Grace stepped aside, just as Harri popped around the corner with Brad close behind.

"Need help?" Harri asked. She focused a stern schoolteacher scowl on Tyler.

"Nope, almost finished," Tyler said.

Grace said, "Dessert was scrumptious, Harri. What

was in that icing?"

"I might tell you the secret some day," Harri said.

Grace nuzzled her dog. "I'll hold you to that. Right now, I really should be heading for home."

"Me, too," Tyler said.

Brad removed his arm from around Harri's waist and took Tyler's outstretched hand.

"Thanks for dinner, Brad," the younger man said. He kissed Harri's cheek. "And thanks for the dessert, Harri."

Harri remained silent.

"I'll walk Grace home," Tyler said.

Harri pulled Grace aside and whispered, "I don't trust him. That man's hiding something."

Grace flicked a glance from the corner of her eyes toward the two men, who were staring at her and Harri. What secrets did Tyler have? Harri could be counted on for her psychic abilities, and Grace knew better than to ignore her warning. Who was he? He said he was from Ohio. Was it possible he'd been sent to find her? Could he be working for Max? The thought made Grace feel as if a giant shovel had scooped out her insides.

"It's a good thing you have Tiffany," Harri said so all could hear. "I've been thinking of getting myself a dog. Did you hear another woman was killed last night?"

Grace's dinner turned to acid, burning her esophagus. She swallowed hard. She'd talked to the police, who'd made her feel foolish for reporting what she'd seen. She'd shrugged it off, but she couldn't stop thinking about the poor women.

Tyler drew his brows together. "Another woman? What happened?"

Harri stared at Tyler, lips pressed together in a thin line. A brief moment of stagnant silence thickened the air. Finally she replied, "Another poor woman was slashed to death by the Knoxville Knifer."

"Another?" Tyler queried.

Harri gave Tyler a look that would make most men worry for their lives.

"Three other victims in the past five weeks," she responded in an accusatory tone. "That makes four women killed by the Knoxville Knifer, and the police don't have a suspect."

"Here in Foxfire?" Tyler asked. He didn't seem to notice Harri's antagonistic attitude.

Brad moved closer to Grace. She gave him a grateful smile for his silent comfort.

"Not here," he answered quickly, placing a hand on Grace's shoulder. "In Knoxville. Nothing bad ever happens in Foxfire."

Gathering strength from Brad's touch, Grace admitted, "I talked to the police today about the latest murder."

Brad frowned. "The police? Did you know that woman?"

"No. But last night I saw someone in the parking garage. He was standing in the shadows beside the elevator on the second floor. The light above the doors was out, but my headlights caught him when I passed. I didn't think much of it until I read the article this morning."

Despite the warmth in the room, she couldn't suppress a shiver. Visions of a knife kept flashing through her mind.

Harri's eyes sparkled with intensity. "You've got to come and let me read the Tarot cards for you. Do you think you saw the Knoxville Knifer?"

"The police don't think so. I couldn't give a very good description. Actually, they made me feel foolish for going in to report it."

Harri squinted, her lips pursing. She shook her head. "Something's going on. You've got something dark corrupting your aura. Come by tomorrow and I'll do a reading."

"Damn it, Harri!" Brad stepped between the two women. "You stop scaring her. She's had enough to deal with the past two days."

Grace put a hand on Brad's arm. "She isn't scaring

me, and besides I believe in Harri's abilities."

Brad shook his head. "I think it's all a bunch of hooey."

Harri glared at Brad. "If you'll get my sweater, I'll be on my way. You're beginning to get on my nerves, Bradley."

"Please don't fight," Grace pleaded. "I'm sure what I saw was nothing at all. Just like the police said."

Harri kept her narrow gaze focused on Brad until he mumbled a brief apology.

Grace kissed Brad and Harri on the cheeks and left them to work out their difference. Tiffany raced ahead, and Tyler soon caught up with her.

"Tiffany," she called. Though she didn't think she had anything to fear from Tyler, one could never be too careful. She felt grateful her dog was near.

Chapter Three

Tyler had to increase his pace to keep up with Grace. Tiffany ran ahead of them, dodging in and out of trees.

Tyler had been following the murders committed by the serial killer dubbed the Knoxville Knifer. At first he wondered if there might be a connection to Max, but discarded the idea because Max preferred a quick kill by shooting his victims in the head. Besides, his list seemed limited to those who'd testified in his trial. Random serial killings didn't fit the profile.

Tyler kept a close surveillance on the wooded area pressing in on them. If Max wasn't here yet, he would be eventually. Tyler intended to be alert and ready. He caught sight of the moonlight glinting off Grace's molten cap of red curls. He took her arm and slowed their pace, not wanting to reach her house too soon.

"You don't have to walk me home," she blurted.

Suppressing a grin, he said, "Maybe not, but I want to. Besides, I have to pass your house to get to mine."

"Just don't get the wrong idea. I'm perfectly capable of taking care of myself."

"Glad to hear that. If a bear shows up, I wouldn't know what to do. Glad you're here to protect me."

Her quick laughter washed over him.

"Brad didn't tell me he was inviting a sexy woman to dinner," he continued.

She looked at him from under one raised eyebrow.

He grinned. "But I'm glad he did."

"You're so full of bull. I suppose women usually throw themselves at your feet."

"Only the four-legged ones."

She grinned and kicked at a stone on the path. "He

29

didn't tell me you were coming either."

"Sneaky, isn't he?"

"Sometimes. Look, Brad is like family. He feels responsible for me." She stopped and swung to face him. "I'm not looking for a relationship. If you want the truth, I've just ended one. I'm not...that is, I've decided..."

He loved the way she moved her hands when she talked, as if leading an invisible orchestra. The top of her head barely reached his shoulder. Her waist was tiny, small enough he felt he could span it with his hands. Below it her hips flared provocatively. Altogether a nice package. One he'd like to sample, if not for his rule against mixing business with pleasure.

Her outstretched arms dropped to her side, and her shoulders sagged. "I'm sorry. I love Brad, but sometimes—"

He cupped her elbow and started walking again. "Hey, don't worry. I'm not looking for a relationship either."

They strolled in silence for several steps. "I must say, that although Brad told me a lot about Harri, she isn't quite what I expected."

Grace's tinkling laugh wrapped around his chest and stole his breath. Something he wasn't prepared for.

"She's a force to be reckoned with. Sometimes her predictions are right on."

"Really? Do you think I should let her read my palm?" He turned her to face him. "Maybe she can tell me if..." He ran his hands up her arms and squeezed her shoulders. "...I'm going to get my wish." He couldn't help pushing her buttons. "You know, make a success of the clinic," he added. He started walking again, slipping his hand back under her elbow.

"Maybe you should," Grace said.

Tyler laughed. "Nah, like Brad, I don't believe in that hokey stuff."

"She might surprise you."

Too quickly they reached her house. She'd left the

porch light on, and he recalled how sexy and vulnerable she'd looked last night standing under its glow, her eyes all red and puffy. He mentally checked his emotions. He couldn't let his feelings get in the way of what he had to do, for he needed to spend more time with her. Even though he hadn't opened for business, he'd have to press her to come to work for him. What a stroke of luck for him that she wasn't employed. "About the job opening—"

Grace pushed her hands out as if to ward him off. "Brad shouldn't have said anything."

"You mean you're not looking for a job?"

She blew out a loud breath. "I am, but—"

He stepped forward and Tiffany plopped herself between them. Her tongue rippled while she panted. He kept his distance, respecting the dog's territorial barrier. "I need an office manager. I don't know what you're looking for, but let's talk."

"I appreciate your offer, but you don't know anything about me."

"I know you can operate a computer. You told me that much. That's why we need to talk. You know, I learn about you, and you learn about..." He winked. "The job opening."

"Let me think about it."

Her eyes sparkled beneath lashes so long and curly he ached to feel them against his skin. The woman was dangerous.

He held out a hand and received a wet kiss from the dog. He loved dogs, but that wasn't the type of kiss he hungered for tonight.

He'd had a few dates over the past few years, but always with women who wouldn't expect a commitment. Something about Grace screamed commitment. Despite the fact she'd been the girlfriend of a mobster, he sensed she might have been telling the jury the truth when she said she didn't know about Max's criminal activities.

But that shouldn't matter. Tyler was here for one reason. To put an end to Max's killing spree and bring the bastard to justice. Or kill him. Whichever opportunity afforded itself. But to have a chance, Tyler needed Grace. If he had to romance her to make that happen, he'd do so and enjoy every second. She wasn't immune to the chemistry boiling between them.

Grace closed her eyes and sent forth an audible sigh. He leaned forward and brushed his lips against hers before she could resist.

He expected a slap, or at the least that she'd push him away. He didn't expect the warm, soft pressure of her lips kissing him back.

Reluctantly, he was the first to pull away. He couldn't do it. No matter what he told himself, he wouldn't be able to use her this way. He wanted to run his fingers through her hair and feel those coppery curls twine around his fingers, and he damned his own weakness. Grace wasn't the kind of woman he could hop into bed with and forget. The last thing he needed was to get involved. One more kiss would lead to big trouble. The kind of trouble he wanted no part of, not now, not ever again.

Tiffany sat on his foot. He stared down at her laughing face. Even the dog knew he lied to himself.

Grace opened her eyes, and damn, that quick he was caught up in wanting to kiss her again.

She tipped her head. A dimple showed in one cheek. She continued to stare at him while her smile rearranged the freckles sprinkled across her cheeks.

"I said I'd think about it," she said.

He couldn't tear his mind away from the throbbing pull of sexual desire. "The kiss?" He touched her cheek.

"No, the job offer."

Quickly she turned, leaving him standing alone staring at her back. Tiffany trotted beside her, and suddenly Tyler wanted to laugh. What a pair. He watched until the door closed, blocking them from his sight.

He ambled home, pondering how quickly his plan had come together. He'd liked the thrill of working for the agency. Would he be able to walk away from it once he'd finished this assignment? Would it absolve him and bring an end to his guilt?

Mulling over the questions wouldn't bring the answers. He had to focus on one thing only. The mission he'd been sent to accomplish.

Having Grace work in the clinic would allow him to keep close tabs on her. She liked animals, and that was a crucial part of establishing trust with customers, so she'd fit in perfectly.

Except for one thing—he wanted to jump her bones.

****

Grace shut the door and knelt to hug Tiffany.

"I'm not doing so well with new beginnings, am I?" She couldn't believe she'd let Tyler kiss her. She didn't even know him. And Harri didn't trust him. She believed in Harri's psychic abilities. And Grace believed in her own intuition. Intuition that told her she'd seen something important in that garage last night.

Tiffany yelped and Grace released her strangle-hold. She hadn't realized how tightly she'd gripped her friend.

"I'm sorry, girl." Grace kissed the dog's nose. "I'm such a ninny for letting myself get spooked. When am I ever going to get over my fear?"

She walked to the bedroom, turning her thoughts to the kiss she'd just shared with Tyler. She had to focus on pleasant thoughts.

She undressed and ran her hands over her breasts, feeling them pebble. She imagined Tyler caressing her, telling her she was beautiful, and making love to her. His kiss still tingled on her lips. She brushed a finger over their fullness. Oh, no doubt about it, Tyler Sandford spelled trouble with a capital T.

Could she work for him?

No way. She'd already made the mistake once of getting involved with her boss. If she accepted a job working for Tyler, she knew she wouldn't be strong enough to resist him.

She put on her robe and went to the kitchen to give Tiffany fresh water.

Staring out the window toward the animal clinic, Grace watched a light blink in the distance and disappear. It reminded her of the legendary foxfire, the strange light that glowed in the wooded mountain range from time to time.

She pulled the curtains to block the view.

Tiffany's nails clicked across the kitchen floor. The clock on the mantle ticked unceasingly. Tick, tock. Tick, tock.

The old house creaked, flexing stiffened joints.

The sounds of the boards settling set her nerves on edge. Too much was happening much too fast. Connor had uncovered her past. If he could do that, then what was to stop her enemies from finding her? She shivered and pulled her robe closer. She might have glimpsed a killer last night, and not so long ago she'd slept with one.

Grace turned out the light. Darkness wrapped her in a black shroud. Harri's words of caution crept into her mind. Grace didn't have a good track record when it came to men, and she trusted Harri's intuition. Was there a connection to the Knoxville Knifer and the man she'd seen?

And what about Tyler? Who was he? Could it be a coincidence that he was from Ohio, too?

Through the crack in the curtain, Grace focused on the darkness that had descended on Foxfire, the community where nothing bad ever happened.

Chapter Four

Adam Shockley walked toward the old Feathers place, which now bore a bright red-lettered sign boasting "Foxfire Animal Clinic." He'd read the ad last weekend announcing the clinic's grand opening.

Passing by Grace Wilkins' cabin, he glanced at the weathered logs and low hanging porch roof. His grandparents had built the house many years ago and it had withstood time with grace and dignity. When he put it up for sale, he scrutinized every prospective buyer. The residents of Foxfire needed to meet a certain criteria. He'd learned that many years ago from his grandfather, and when his grandfather died, followed by the death of Adam's father, the responsibility passed down to Adam.

When Grace had placed an offer on the house, he'd told the realtor he needed to meet the prospective buyer before committing. The moment he'd met Grace, all his reservations fell away. An angel, beautiful and sweet, she added a spark of life to Foxfire.

He'd learned from Brad that she'd broken off her engagement and was no longer working for the District Attorney's office. It was time to make his move. He'd invite her to dinner. Women liked to be courted. And flowers. He'd have to remember flowers. His pace picked up, encouraged by his decision. He squinted under the sun's glare and adjusted his ball cap lower.

When he reached his destination, he was happy to see a new coat of white paint brightened the old two-story house. Adam hoped this business would be good for the community. His family had owned a big portion of this mountain for many generations, and he had to protect his heritage.

Adam turned the knob and pushed open the door, setting off a clanging. He smiled at the cowbell on a chain, admiring the simplicity of the country-inspired welcome. Foxfire was a community that remained true to its Appalachian roots, and it looked like the vet planned to follow the culture. He'd even heard rumors he would make house calls.

"Hi. Can I help you?"

Adam swiveled his head. He grinned at the man who stared back at him. Adam felt dwarfed, though he stood nearly six-feet tall. The man smiled back, lines crinkling at the edges of his intense green eyes.

"Nice touch." Adam nodded at the bell then extended his hand. "I'm Adam Shockley."

"Tyler Sandford."

"I've been watching progress on the clinic." Adam perused the open area of the reception room with the two wooden benches against one wall, which reminded him of the pews in the Baptist church he'd attended as a child. "You did a good job with the remodeling."

Tyler swept his left arm in a welcoming gesture. "Would you like a tour? I'm proud of how well it all came together."

"Quite a change from when old Charlie owned it."

"You knew the former owner?"

Adam nodded. "Born and raised in these parts. I used to buy peanuts from a stand out by the road. That's how Charlie passed the time after his wife, Leona, died. He never went out much after that, except for church on Sunday. I think he grieved himself to death."

"Sad." Tyler pushed open the door to the examination room and ushered Adam in. "You probably know most of the people around here."

"Yep. Most."

Tyler leaned against the stainless steel table and crossed his ankles. "Do you think I have a snowball's chance in hell of making a success of this clinic?"

"Maybe. Depends on what you mean by success."

Adam narrowed his gaze on Tyler, taking his measure. He appeared to be about ten years younger than Adam's forty-two years. He wore the local uniform of jeans and a pocket t-shirt, but an open white lab coat topped it.

Tyler met his gaze directly, man-to-man, with no sign of uncertainty. "I've got pictures of Norman Rockwell in my head. It's the main reason I decided to set up practice away from the city. I'm excited about the prospect of making house calls, just like the old timers did."

He pushed his body off the table and led the way through a door to the back area filled with cages.

"My idea of success is to make enough to keep the place running and put food on the table."

Adam laughed. "Then you shouldn't have a problem. That is..." He turned to face Tyler. "If you're serious about making house calls from time to time."

Tyler's lips lifted in a grin. "I'm serious."

Adam nodded.

Tyler showed him the rest of the clinic and the living quarters he'd set up for himself. By the time Adam left, he felt comfortable that the new clinic would be perfect for Foxfire. He'd make a few calls, and soon Tyler would have the community's support.

He whistled and retraced his steps, stopping when he reached Grace's house.

Tiffany raced toward him with her ears laid back. She came to an abrupt halt in front of him. Her lips pulled up over her teeth and she emitted a low growl.

He hated dogs. Ever since that one had bitten his leg and drew blood, he'd kept his distance. He wished Grace wouldn't let this one run loose. But he hadn't heard of the dog biting anybody. He held out his hand. Maybe if he could make friends with it...

"Come here, girl. I won't hurt you."

But the dog remained steadfast, blocking the path, warning him not to move closer.

"Tiffany! Bad girl."

With relief, Adam turned his gaze to the beauty

walking across the leaf-strewn yard.

"I'm sorry," Grace said. She walked up and grabbed the dog's collar. "I don't know why she's acting this way. She's usually very friendly."

Adam gulped. Grace's hair ignited in the sunshine. The curls rioted in flames of red and gold. Her beauty froze him, driving the words he wanted to say clear down to his toes. He pulled the cap a little lower.

Grace gazed at him quizzically. "Are you all right?"

He stepped forward with his hand extended toward her dog. "I was trying to make friends with her."

Tiffany sniffed at his fingers and rumbled another low growl.

"Shame on you, Tiff," Grace scolded.

"She's just protecting you. That's not a bad thing."

Grace grinned and his stomach wrenched.

"Were you down at the clinic, Adam?" Grace asked.

"Yeah. Just checking it out. The new vet seems okay."

"Tiffany likes him. Don't you?" Grace ruffled the dog's fur.

Adam's heart nose-dived. She'd already met the vet? What chance did he have against the younger, good-looking man? But looks weren't everything. And his age gave him the maturity that a woman like Grace needed. He had to make his move now.

"Grace. I was wondering..."

She lifted a hand to shade her eyes.

"Would you have dinner with me?" he blurted. He stuffed his hands in his pockets, rocked back on his heels and waited for her answer. She hesitated for a moment, and his heart missed a beat. Emotions he couldn't read played across her face. He rocked back and forth to keep from bolting.

"Sure, Adam. Maybe we can do that sometime."

"Tomorrow night?"

Her face turned pink. "Not tomorrow night. I'm sorry."

Adam kicked a clod of dirt, wishing he could kick something else. Something substantial that would bring a feeling of satisfaction. Like the dog.

Tiffany growled, then barked a warning.

"Tiffany. No." Grace turned her dazzling deep blue eyes up to meet his gaze. "I'm sorry. Maybe some other time?"

Some other time. Sure. Like she meant that. He could tell she wasn't interested in spending time with the likes of him.

"Yeah. Another time," Adam muttered.

She tugged Tiffany's collar and pulled her toward the house. "See you later."

He watched her walk away, her hips swaying hypnotically. She couldn't put him off forever. He'd find a way to get to her, make her notice him and see he'd be a good catch. He had a lot to offer a woman like Grace.

Perhaps he'd get his hair cut. Maybe change the way he dressed. There had to be a way to catch her eye.

****

Connor flexed his fingers, loosening the tension riddling his nerves. Sweat beaded his forehead. When he'd made the decision to run for state senator, not once had he feared adverse publicity. Now he lived with that constant worry.

His connection at the police station had told him about Grace's visit. He needed her to stay away from Knoxville until he came up with a way to handle the publicity their broken engagement would cause. He hadn't figured on Grace running off, nor on her quitting her job.

He'd thought he had her figured out, but she'd shown more spunk than he thought she possessed. She'd managed to keep her past a secret from him. Now he had to make it stay hidden from anything that could damage his political career. Too bad, for he'd thought she'd make a perfect wife. She'd been quietly aloof and had presented herself well to the media. Now he had to find a way to extricate himself without risking negative press.

He listened to the third ring on the phone line. Where was she? He loosened his tie and unfastened his collar button. If she didn't answer—

"Hello?"

He stopped pacing. The sound of Grace's voice, soft and breathless, stirred desire that warred with his anger.

God help him, he still wanted her.

"Grace. I have to see you. It's important." Connor sank into his leather office chair and toyed with the folder on his desk.

"There's nothing more for us to talk about."

He picked up a pencil and tapped it on the desk. "You've still got a key to the office and you left some personal items in your desk. Let's meet for lunch and we can exchange things."

Silence met his ear.

"Grace?"

"I'll mail the key...anything I left in the desk you can throw away."

"It's just lunch, Grace. Nothing more. I'm not going to try and talk you into coming back to work. I have something important that I need to tell you, but I can't do it over the phone. Meet me Toby's Diner. Twelve-thirty sharp."

"No."

"Grace—"

The dial tone hummed in his ear. He pressed the off button and threw the cell phone onto his desk. He'd managed to squelch the story on her police report. Thank goodness for his connections. But he couldn't keep things buried forever. Not if she kept showing up, creating speculations he couldn't afford. He snatched his jacket from the back of his chair. If the bitch wouldn't come to him, he'd go to her.

****

Grace stormed from the house with Tiffany on her heels. How dare Connor order her around after telling her she wasn't good enough for him? Connor was scum. Worse than a bottom-feeding catfish.

She stomped along the path, each step fueling her anger.

Tiffany sniffed and clawed at a rock, which Grace picked up and flung into the woods.

"Come on, Tiff. Let's go see about a job." She hadn't seen the new clinic yet anyway. A week had passed since the night she'd promised to think about the job offer, and she hadn't found another job. So what if she found Tyler attractive? He said he wasn't looking for a relationship either. Worse came to worst, they'd have an affair. It wouldn't be the end of the world. As long as neither of them expected more than that, no one would be hurt.

Tiffany pushed her nose into the dirt, pulled her snout back and sneezed.

Grace laughed and Tiffany lowered her front legs into a playful crouch. Grace bent forward, hands extended.

Tiffany whirled and ran.

Grace followed for a few feet, and then stopped.

Tiffany changed directions and zipped past Grace, barking with playful glee. Grace ran after her, coming to a breathless halt at the clinic. She placed her hands on her thighs and leaned over to catch her breath.

The dog barked, tail wagging rapidly.

"Come on, Tiff." Grace climbed the stairs and opened the clinic door. A bell jangled, announcing their arrival.

Tyler swiveled away from a computer to face them, a frown pulling his eyebrows together. When he saw who'd entered, he stood and a smile smoothed his face, igniting a flame in the emerald depths of his eyes.

"Grace." He walked toward her. "Are you here to see the clinic, or is Tiffany sick?"

Tiffany leaped at the sound of her name and placed her front paws on his chest, tongue flicking toward his face.

Tyler wasn't fast enough to avoid a doggy kiss.

"Down, Tiff," Grace ordered. "I'm sorry. She seems to

have forgotten all her behavior training."

Tiffany dropped to all fours, but her eyes remained focused on Tyler.

Tyler stroked her head. "It's good to see you too, girl." He grinned at Grace. "She doesn't look sick. Does that mean you came to see me?" He wiggled his eyebrows comically.

"We came to see the clinic. After all, when it comes to Tiffany, I can't be too careful. I can't trust her care to just any old veterinarian who shows up on my doorstep."

He laughed. "Fair enough." He glanced at his watch. "Next patient is due in an hour. Let me give you a tour, then maybe you'll take pity on me. If you hadn't shown up, I might have thrown that damn computer out the back door."

Grace followed Tyler into an examining room. Her gaze took in the stainless steel monster scale Brad had mentioned. "Brad wasn't kidding. That thing probably could weigh a bear."

"Tiff, hop up." Tyler patted the scale.

Tiffany put her front paws on, then backed off.

Grace laughed, beginning to feel more at ease. "She's a true female. Doesn't want to reveal her weight."

Tyler hoisted the dog to the scale and adjusted the weights on the balance bar. "Ninety pounds on the nose."

Tiffany wagged her tail and barked.

Grace and Tyler laughed in unison.

"She's a great dog," Tyler said.

"She's my best friend."

Tyler rested a hand on Grace's shoulder and squeezed gently. "She's lucky."

A tingle ran down her arm. So much for hoping she could remain distant from this man. He turned her on.

Tiffany put her nose to the crack at the bottom of a closed door and whined. A paw snuck under the door and tapped against Tiffany's nose.

"How's Tiffany with cats?" Tyler asked.

"Cats?" Grace didn't have much experience with

felines, but she supposed she'd have to get used to them if she worked here.

Tyler nodded at the furry paw stretched beneath the door. "That's Muffin. She walked in about a week ago and made herself at home. I advertised, but no one's claimed her yet."

Tyler opened the door and a fat, fluffy, amber-striped cat pranced in, head held high, tail straight in the air. A little crook at the end resembled a fishhook. Muffin rubbed between Tiffany's front legs, weaving a figure eight.

Tiffany scrambled backwards.

Muffin appeared bored and jumped to the examination table. She began to groom away the dog germs.

Grace ran her hand down the cat's back, marveling at the silky thickness. Muffin stopped, tongue poking out, one paw raised. She stared deeply into Grace's eyes for a moment and then returned to the task of grooming. It left Grace with a strange feeling. Almost as if the cat could read her mind.

Tiffany leaned heavily against Grace's legs, begging for attention.

"Are you jealous?" Grace asked. She rubbed the dog's ears and looked at Tyler. "I'm surprised she's being so calm. She loves to chase animals outside."

"Ah, but Muffin isn't an animal. She's a queen reborn. Can't you tell?"

Muffin leaped to the counter, then to the top of the supply cabinets. She gazed down at them, then curled into a ball and tucked her golden eyes behind one paw.

"See what I mean? She acts like she owns the place."

"Wonder where she came from?"

Tyler shrugged. "Beats me."

Grace looked through the open door at the cages lined against the wall in the room behind them.

"Come on." Tyler led them into the large area. "This is the boarding room. Not for sick animals, but for those whose families are out of town for a few days. Of course, the cages are just to keep them safe at night. There's an open fenced area behind the house where they can run and play during the day."

"So you plan on boarding animals, too?"

"Absolutely. If you can't trust your vet, who can you trust?" He winked boldly. "Come on, I'll show you my apartment."

Her mind screamed danger, but her legs carried her up the stairs behind him. The warmth of Tyler's apartment surprised and pleased Grace. He'd taken care to make the rooms a home, not just a place to sleep. She'd expected buttery soft leather furniture, not the deep blue sofa with throw pillows piled high. Pictures of mountain scenery graced the newly painted ivory walls.

He opened the door to his bedroom, where she spied a hand-stitched quilt in shades of green covering the massive wooden bed. She could imagine falling into the softness of the mattress with him beside her. She felt her face flame when his glance caught hers.

"Like it?" he asked.

She backed out of the door and into the living room. "It's...nice," she squeaked out. She cleared her throat. "We'd better get back and check on Tiffany. That cat might decide to have her for lunch."

Tyler's expression told her he wasn't fooled. He knew what she'd been thinking.

He finished the tour by showing her the converted garage that had been turned into a care unit, complete with a sick bay area and two incubator-type units on wheels. They ended back in the reception area.

"And this," Tyler pointed at a computer, "is the piece of crap that's driving me insane." He scratched his head. "I've been trying to get the billing set up for two blasted days. The program said it was user-friendly, but I don't think it likes me." He shook his head. "I'm writing patient bills on pieces of notebook paper."

"Maybe I can help. I know a little about software

programs. Do you want me to try?"

"If you can get the damn billing program to work, you'll earn the biggest and juiciest steak money can buy."

"You're on." She sat in front of the computer and began to tap the keyboard. She felt his gaze fastened on her, but she managed to ignore the urge to turn and look at him. Finally, he left her alone. She studied the instruction booklet and soon lost herself in the work.

She had the program functioning when the doorbell jangled. She spared a quick glance as Tyler came from the back room and greeted a woman with a pet carrier. He led her to the examination room. The door shut behind them and their voices faded.

Grace looked through the appointment book and entered the names of the clients he'd penciled in. She tested the program by printing a bogus bill and shot her fist in the air when it worked. She loved the feeling of success.

A few minutes later, the elderly woman came out. She placed a carrier on the counter. Inside was one of the biggest cats Grace had ever seen.

"Tinkerbell's good for another year, Mrs. Engleworth." Tyler handed Grace a folder.

Grace snatched it, trying to hide her smile. *Tinkerbell?*

"How much do I owe you, Tyler?" Mrs. Engleworth fluttered her eyelashes in a shameless display that brought Grace one step closer to dissolving in laughter. The woman was older than Brad, for crying out loud.

Tyler, however, winked at the woman and then grinned at Grace. "Seventeen for the booster shots and twenty for the exam."

"Got it," Grace said. She printed out an invoice and handed it to Mrs. Engleworth.

Tyler's eyes widened with appreciative surprise, and Grace suppressed a grin.

The woman wrote out a check while the mean looking tomcat, so inappropriately named, glared at Grace with feral green eyes. Its tiger-striped fur dusted the air as it swung its tail, flicking the sides of the cage.

Tiffany pushed to her feet, stretched and grunted, then trotted over and lifted her nose toward the carrier.

A long paw extended through the bars, baring long needle-sharp claws. The cat hissed.

"No, Tiff," Grace admonished. The dog gave a sorrowful look and went back to her spot on the floor. Muffin jumped onto the counter and the two cats began a slapping match.

"Sorry," Grace said. She lifted Muffin and placed her on the floor.

Tyler winked, then walked Mrs. Engleworth to the door. "Thanks for bringing Tinkerbell in." He opened the door.

"Thank you, Doctor."

"You're welcome. So long, Tinkerbell." He closed the door and turned a beaming smile on Grace. "You're hired."

"What about the steak?" she teased.

"You earned it, and I always keep my promises. I'm also offering you a job as my office manager, slash receptionist, slash billing clerk. The pay's not great, but the boss is a great guy."

"Not so fast. What are you willing to pay?"

His grin stretched his cheeks. "We can work it out. If you don't like the salary, maybe we can work out some additional benefits."

"Only if you're talking about health insurance," Grace countered. She knew he was flirting with her, and it felt good, like she was a normal person with no dark secrets.

He laughed. "Grace, it's going to be a lot of fun working with you."

"Salary?" she prompted.

"How about twelve dollars an hour to start with a raise when business picks up."

"Deal." She held out her hand. "When do I get the steak?"

Tyler sandwiched her hand between his, sending warm currents up her arm and into her stomach. "Tonight. I'll pick you up at six. And dress casual." He gave a lop-sided grin.

Muffin pranced into the room and leaped gracefully into the chair Grace had vacated.

They laughed when Tiffany, who'd been lying on the floor, scrambled to get out of her way.

Grace left the clinic floating on a cloud of euphoria, but it took a nosedive when she noticed the car in her driveway. The dark blue Jaguar looked out of place and so did the angry face of the man behind the wheel.

Connor.

Chapter Five

"We need to talk, Grace." Connor slammed the door on the Jaguar and walked toward her.

Tiffany growled and the hair bristled on her neck.

He stopped. "Keep the dog away from me."

"You're trespassing. She's protecting me."

Connor threw up his hands. "Protecting you? God, Grace, I'd never hurt you. You know that."

He took another step in her direction, and Grace grabbed Tiffany's collar. "You'd better stay back, Connor. She's trained to attack and I'm not sure I can control her."

Connor's face blanched. He glanced uneasily at the growling dog. "Look, can we go inside and talk for a few minutes?"

"No. Say whatever you came to say. Then leave."

Connor's eyes narrowed. A muscle jumped along his jaw. Finally, he relaxed his stance and backed toward the car. He leaned against the door, his feet crossed at the ankles. His lustful gaze swept her from head to toe.

Why had she thought she could marry this egotistical clod? She knew he'd never loved her. And, God help her, at one time she'd been willing to settle. She'd wanted the dream more than anything.

"You're as beautiful as ever, Grace. I miss you."

"Too little, too late."

"Admit it, honey. You miss me, too. We had a good thing going. It doesn't have to end, you know. I have a proposition." He waved his hand in the direction of the cabin. "We don't have to part ways completely. We can meet here where no one will see us. What do you say?"

Grace gritted her teeth to keep her tongue from spitting out every curse word she'd ever learned. Connor seemed to take her silence as a positive sign.

"I'll make it worth your while."

That did it. "You know what, Connor? You can take your sleazy proposal elsewhere. I'm not interested in anything you have to offer."

"Given your past, you should be glad I'm still interested."

She wanted to drive her fist into his sneering face. Tiffany tugged, straining to break free. Connor smiled his toothy lawyer smile and Grace was tempted to let go. She took a step toward him with a smile pasted on her face.

Connor straightened and held out his arms.

God, he actually expected her to throw herself into his embrace. "I'm not for sale, Connor. You've got to the count of three to get in your car and leave. Otherwise, I turn my dog loose."

Tiffany lunged, and Grace's arm jerked. "Good girl," she said.

"You never used to be so particular."

Fury ignited her. "You know nothing. Your mind is a cesspool. One—"

"All right. I'm going." Red anger suffused his face. Connor wasn't a graceful loser, neither in nor out of the courtroom. "But you better think over the offer. I doubt you'll find another as generous."

"Two—"

"And don't talk to the press. About anything! Your little fiasco at the police station shows just how off-balance you are. I think the media will sympathize with me when I tell them how devastated I was to learn you're a drug addict."

"Tell them anything you want. Your threats can't hurt me."

He sneered. "You don't know how powerful I am."

"Three." Grace released her hold on Tiffany's collar.

If she hadn't been so angry, she'd have laughed at Connor's scrambling slide into the sports car. He bumped his head against the roof and pulled the door closed.

Tiffany reached the car just as the door slammed shut. She jumped, paws clicking loudly against the window. Then she dropped, clawing the rich paint as she slid to the ground.

Connor revved the engine and rolled down the window.

"Bitch," he yelled.

With a growl Tiffany lunged, and the window quickly closed. The dog trotted back to Grace, tail wagging proudly.

Grace looked with satisfaction at the deep scratches in the Jaguar's perfect paint job. Tires spun in the gravel. Connor turned the car around and sped away.

When his car was out of sight, Grace laughed. She felt victorious.

Tiffany sped off into the woods, turned and ran back.

Grace grabbed the dog's face and leaned down to stare into Tiffany's eyes. "Good girl. That deserves a treat."

Walking to the house, she fought the desire to look over her shoulder. The hairs prickled on the back of her neck, making her feel certain someone was watching her. Spider legs crawled her spine, until she could stand it no longer. She spun around.

Adam stood on the path, a solitary figure between two overshadowing pine trees. Only the grim set of his lips were visible beneath the lowered ball cap. The air changed as if a huge cloud hovered above. She forced a smile.

"Hi, Adam."

"If that man gives you any more trouble, you just let me know."

She stared at his shadowed face. "Thanks."

"We take care of our own around here." His lips turned up in a brief smile before he trudged up the hill toward his house.

Grace mounted the steps and came to an abrupt halt.

A single red rose lay on the welcome mat.

She stared at the perfect red bud, round and plump and clinging to the end of a green thorny stem. It looked out of place on the rough weave of the mat. She turned to look for Adam but he was already out of sight.

Grace picked up the flower and carried it inside and filled a glass with water. She put the lonely bloom into its depth. Adam must have left the rose. It was too much of a coincidence that he'd been present for the scene with Connor. Poor Adam. He must have waited for her to return and find his gift. She sensed his loneliness and could even empathize. Maybe she should have dinner with him. She'd have to make him understand they could only be friends, though. He was much too old for her—nearly old enough to be her father—and he certainly didn't seem the romantic type.

If Tyler gave her a rose, it would be romantic, but coming from Adam it just seemed sad.

Grace sighed. She wanted a man who'd take control in a wild, wonderful way. Someone who'd make her knees knock, and fireworks explode when they kissed. She wanted a strong man, one who was sure of himself, one not afraid to admit his love. She wanted a man like the ones in her romance novels, one with a broad chest, muscled arms, and a to-die-for wicked smile. She wanted a man who'd protect her, yet respect her strength, and not hold her past against her.

Reluctantly, she acknowledged that Tyler looked the part. A vision of broad shoulders and flashing green eyes made shivers run up her thighs. But she wouldn't let him get under her skin. Not even if he *could* model for the cover of one of the romance novels she loved.

No way would she settle again. She'd rather live the rest of her life single. She'd made a home here in Foxfire with Brad, Harri, and Tiffany. Her family.

She didn't need a man. Grace reached for her key ring. She would rid herself of any further contact with Connor. With a muttered curse, she left the house and started her car. She'd hand off the key and be finished

51

with him forever.

Twenty minutes later, she entered his office. Sarah, the receptionist, gaped open-mouthed at her. "Grace. I thought—"

Grace knew Sarah had the hots for Connor. She'd be making a play for him soon, if she hadn't already. As far as Grace was concerned, she was welcome to him.

"Don't panic, I'm not coming back to work." Grace handed her the key. "Just give this to Connor."

Sarah accepted it, a frown line appearing between her brows.

"And tell him where I go and who I talk to is none of his business anymore."

Grace pushed through the door. She rounded the corner and plowed into a man's hard chest. His hands closed around her arms, steadying her.

"Whoa," he said.

"I'm sorry." She pulled free and met his gaze. A prickle of unease skittered up her spine when she stared into his deep-set sable eyes. The skin pulled taught on his angular face giving it the look of an actor who'd had too many face-lifts. The suit he wore looked expensive. Grace felt a prickle of unfounded fear. Where had she seen this guy before? Something about his voice and his eyes seemed vaguely familiar.

"Sorry," she muttered, pulling free from his grasp.

His lips turned upward in a friendly gesture, though his eyes remained cold and hard.

She suppressed a shudder and stepped around him to push the button for the elevator. The doors opened and Grace stepped inside. She pressed the lobby button and risked a glance between the closing doors. The man gave a slow wink. Sweat beaded her forehead. She stepped aside, breathing deeply of the suddenly stagnant air. Relief coursed through her when the elevator began its descent.

****

Grace was sitting on the porch enjoying the view when Tyler walked into the clearing. His polo shirt hugged his broad shoulders, the deep green enhancing those emerald sparks in his eyes. Much to her surprise, he wore the dirty tennis shoes he'd had on the first night she met him.

He followed her gaze down to his feet, then gave her a big grin. "Hey, they're comfortable and perfect for hiking."

"Hiking? Why didn't you drive?"

"Drive?" He looked puzzled, and then suddenly his face lit with understanding. "I should have made myself clear. I'm cooking steaks on the grill." He shrugged. "I bought the biggest rib-eyes I could find. And my homemade marinade can't be beat."

Oh, Lord. Trouble. Having dinner in a restaurant was one thing, but how would she manage an entire evening alone with him? "Oh."

He laughed. "Don't sound so skeptical. I promise not to poison you."

There went that wicked smile sending fireflies swarming through her stomach. Tyler gripped her hand and pulled her to her feet. They walked toward the clinic. "Things are different here, but I like the slow pace of living," he said.

Grace smiled up at him. "That's why I moved here. I wanted to get away from the hustle and bustle of the city."

"What city?"

Uh-oh. She had to watch her words. Working with Tyler was going to pose more problems than her attraction to him. "A not-so-nice suburb of St. Louis, Missouri. I had to learn early how to protect myself."

Tyler squeezed her upper arm, grinning mischievously. "You've got a set of muscles all right."

"Trust me, it takes more than physical strength to survive the streets. You've got to be mentally tough and not show any sign of fear. Otherwise, they'll chew you up."

"They?"

"The streets."

"Do your parents still live in Missouri?"

"I don't have a clue where my Dad is. He left before I was born."

"And your mother?"

"She's dead."

"I'm sorry." Tyler gazed compassionately down at her.

"Don't be. She's been gone a long time."

They finished the walk in silence and Tyler led her up a flight of stairs to a wooden deck where heat emanated from the gas grill beside sliding doors opening to his kitchen.

He retrieved a platter and placed the meat on the grill. "I figured we could share with Tiffany."

Grace laughed. "I fed her before we came. I don't give her table scraps. You're a vet. Don't you recommend high-priced dog food, and give lectures on the perils of people food?"

"Nope. I believe in spoiling."

They chatted about the proper way to raise pets while Tyler tended the steaks.

He hadn't exaggerated. They were mouth-wateringly perfect. Baked potatoes, salad and wine completed the meal. When they'd cleared the dishes, they sat in chairs on the deck. Gas torches flickered, giving a romantic glow to the growing dusk.

"How long have you lived here?" Tyler asked.

"Three years."

Tyler put his feet on the railing. "I think I'm going to like it. When I was a kid, we lived in a small town where everybody knew everybody else's business. Back then I hated it. Couldn't wait to get away. Then after college I couldn't wait to get back."

"Then why did you leave? What brought you to Foxfire?"

He winked at her. "The scenery, what else?" He stood and leaned his elbows on the railing, gazing out into the trees. "Even at night, it's beautiful."

That was the second time he'd avoided revealing the reason he'd moved to Foxfire. Harri's words came back to her that Tyler was hiding something. But Grace shrugged it off. Nothing about Tyler seemed threatening. Besides, everyone had secrets to guard.

Tiffany yawned loudly.

Grace mirrored Tyler's stance, leaning over the railing. "Did you know that sometimes you can see foxfire glowing along the ground?"

"I thought that was a legend. It's true then? Have you ever seen it?"

She nodded. "It's beautiful and haunting at the same time." His shoulder brushed hers. A shiver crawled up her spine.

He draped an arm around her shoulders and pulled her closer. "Are you cold? Do you want to go inside for a while?"

His hand caressed her arm. Goosebumps arose that had nothing at all to do with being chilled.

"I'm not cold. I love being outside. We have one thing in common. I moved here for the mountain scenery and serenity, too."

He turned her to face him. "*And* we both love animals. We seem to have a lot in common." His thumbs caressed her cheeks.

Her heart tripped faster. His nostrils did that little flare thing again, which she found totally sensuous.

"That's true." Her voice came out an octave higher than usual. She cleared her throat.

He lifted her and sat her on the railing facing him. She placed her hands on his shoulders for balance. Her whole body felt as if it were melting. Like the witch in *The Wizard of Oz*, soon she'd be nothing but a puddle at his feet.

"So when do we see this foxfire?" he asked.

Small talk, she told herself. Focus on the small talk, not on his face. Not on the way the torches add highlights to his dark hair. Not on the fact that his arms surrounded her, resting on either side of her hips.

"Only when the moon is full and the night is bright."

"Ah, unlike tonight." He gazed up at the sky where clouds hid most of the stars.

She stared at the expanse of his neck and the dark hairs that had escaped the neckline of his shirt. "Too overcast," she said.

He lowered his head and stared at her. Not just stared but *stared*. The message in his eyes tapped on her heart.

He brushed a knuckle under her chin.

"You're beautiful."

She fought against the growing attraction. She couldn't.handle an affair with this guy. He'd eat her alive.

She tried to jump down, but his hands spanned her waist pulsing heat waves through her body. The jump turned into a slow body slide. Her hands gripped his shoulders a little tighter. Her breath caught in her throat. Her toes touched the deck at the same moment she felt his arousal.

Her head spun, sending her closer against his chest. His arms closed around her. Her heart and mind battled and her heart won.

She parted her lips and suddenly they were pressed against his. He took the kiss deeper, his hands sliding upward, thumbs brushing the sides of her breasts. It wasn't enough. She wanted more. Needed more. Ached for his intimate touch.

She ran her hands through his collar-length hair, loving the feel of the silky thick strands. His tongue teased her, begging and offering more.

****

Tyler wanted to scoop her up and carry her to his bed. His thumbs circled the soft flesh of her breasts, emboldened by her passionate response. He flicked his tongue against her lips and she opened, accepting his advance. A little voice whispered that he shouldn't be doing this, but he ignored it, giving in to the hunger of the moment.

Someone moaned. He thought it was her, but it might have been him. He pulled her closer, caught up in a heart-pounding desire that burned higher with every passing second.

Her passion overwhelmed him, sucking him into a swirling vortex. She said she didn't want another relationship. Neither did he. Yet, here he was, all wrapped up in Grace Wilkins. Surprise, surprise.

He stepped backward taking her with him until a sharp painful yip stopped him. "What the—" He sidestepped, trying to maintain their balance.

Grace shoved against his chest, her eyes round and dilated, frightened like a deer caught in the headlights. He read the feeling of panic in her gaze. He didn't believe what had happened any more than she did. He should be thankful for small favors, because if it hadn't been for the dog, he'd have ripped off Grace's clothes and sated his long suppressed sexual desires. The electricity pulsing between them nearly sparked in the dark.

Grace knelt beside Tiffany, stroking her fur. "Poor baby. Are you all right," she murmured.

He closed his eyes and dropped his head back. Damn, what poor timing.

Things had escalated so fast. One moment he'd been talking about the legendary foxfire, the next he'd been on fire for Grace. And the flames still seared him. Over the blood pounding through his head, he tried to grab hold of reason. The woman was dangerous. He'd come here to do a job—one that didn't include seducing Grace Wilkins.

He knelt to check the dog for injuries. The bulge against his zipper grew tighter and more painful. Obviously unscathed, Tiffany leaped up, knocking him on his butt. Her tail wagged in wild abandon.

Grace gave a short laugh, then clapped her hand over her mouth.

He looked at her. She licked her swollen lips, which did nothing to ease his tortured libido. The torches played softly across the sprinkle of freckles on her nose. Whatever hold she had on him wasn't letting go. He could see in her eyes that she'd regained control. He had to do the same. He'd come to Foxfire to forget, not to get involved. "I'm sorry," he said.

"It was an accident. Tiffany's not hurt." She pushed to her feet.

"I wasn't talking about the damn dog!"

She placed her hands on those curvy hips. "She has a name. *Tiffany.*" Her chin jerked higher, pointing at him in an accusatory manner. "And she's not a damn dog."

He felt like an idiot sitting on the deck arguing with the woman he'd nearly undressed.

Tiffany licked his face, further deflating his libido. "Yeah," he said. He pushed Tiffany's head away from his face. "She's a great dog."

He met Grace's gaze. "I'm sorry about...you know, trying to ravage you."

"Ravage? Do you read romance novels or what?" She glared down at him. "We kissed. That's all. People kiss all the time. Forget about it. I already have."

Forget? Was she kidding? He'd remember every pleasurable second of that kiss. He still wanted to make love to her. How in the world would he be able to look at her day in and day out and keep his hands off?

The torches flickered, casting a shadow across her face. What secrets did she hide behind those beautiful blue eyes? He sensed she'd been hurt, and that connected with a nerve deep inside. His own hurt ran deep and it still cut at him, slicing his gut like a piece of broken glass. Guilt rode his dreams at night. Sometimes he thought he'd never be able to forget, to forgive.

He knew most of her secrets, or at least the worst of them. And he meant to protect her while he used her to get what he wanted. Getting emotionally involved was not an option.

His plans had been to bury himself in the mountains and his work, but he hadn't planned on finding Grace

Wilkins so tempting. Nor had he planned on her having the power to open his wounds again.

"You expect me to forget that kiss?" he asked, giving her a wink.

She glared at him. "I do. And if anyone should apologize it's me. I took advantage of *you*."

He forced a grin. "Grace, you didn't take advantage of me. From the moment I laid eyes on you, I thought you were the sexiest woman I'd ever seen. Having you here, all alone, well I couldn't resist." He stood and shoved his hands in his pockets. "But I promise to keep my hands to myself from now on."

Was that regret he saw in her eyes or only his wishful thinking? Tyler glanced at his watch. "It's getting late. Tomorrow's a working day for both of us."

Grace dusted her bottom. "You're right. I should be going."

"I'll walk you home."

"No need. Tiffany and I'll be fine."

"Humor me." He followed her down the steps. "My mother taught me to be a gentleman. I open doors for women, lift heavy packages, and always walk my dates to their door."

"It wasn't a date, Tyler."

He let her keep the illusion. When they reached her cabin, he waited until she opened the door and flipped on a light.

She turned to face him. "Thanks for dinner."

"You're welcome."

She started to close the door, but he called out. "Grace?"

"Yes?"

"Be sure to lock your door."

Chapter Six

Torture. No other word could describe the agony of being near Tyler while maintaining what Grace hoped was a professional demeanor. Would this day never end? Each time she met his eyes, her lungs squeezed out every bit of air, leaving her feeling as if she'd just run a long-distance marathon.

Yet, Tyler didn't seem the least bit affected. He'd given her a lab coat, much too large, and laughed after she slipped it on and it hung to her knees. He smiled each time he handed her a patient's chart, and if his heart beat faster when their hands accidentally touched, his expression didn't show it. She supposed she should be grateful.

All morning, she created new patient files, diligently entered information into the computer, collected payments, and chatted with pet owners. She handled dogs and cats of all sizes, including Muffin, who was determined to sit on the mouse pad and stare at the cursor flicking across the monitor.

By the end of the day, Grace could hardly wait to get home. Tiffany ran off toward Brad's, but Grace had no such intentions. All she wanted was to eat a salad, read the paper, pay her bills, and go to bed. Tomorrow being Saturday, she'd only have to endure the torture for a few hours. Somehow she needed to forget about that kiss. Tyler obviously had.

He'd been all business, never once even hinting that he found her attractive, or sexy, or irresistible. That's what really upset her. Not that she wanted him to, of course, but he had said he'd never forget.

She fixed a salad and opened the newspaper. One

look at the headline had her coughing and spitting sweetened tea across the print. There on the front page was a picture of her and Connor. She recognized it as one taken at a fundraiser they'd attended several weeks ago. Connor smiled into the camera, his arm draped possessively across her shoulders. The headline read "What's the Verdict, Counselor?" She scanned the article, which questioned why the two of them hadn't been seen in public together lately. They reported that she no longer worked for the D.A.'s office, and Connor had been spotted having dinner with another woman.

She smiled. Connor must be seething. Sooner or later he'd have to fabricate a story of why they'd split. The humor of his dilemma filled Grace with malicious glee. Let him say derogatory things about her. She could care less. Years ago she'd been branded by the press. They couldn't hurt her now. It would serve Connor right if they learned the truth about her past.

She finished her salad and skimmed the rest of the paper before Tiffany scrambled her way through the pet door.

"Are you hungry?" Grace set the paper aside. A tapping on the door startled her until she heard Brad's voice.

"How was your first day at the clinic?" he asked, entering the room.

"Fine." Grace filled Tiffany's bowl, then reached for a glass from the cabinet. "Tea?"

Brad pulled out a chair and seated himself. "No coffee?"

"I can brew a pot."

He waved a hand. "Don't bother. Tea's fine. Where'd you get the rose?"

"Adam."

Brad scrunched his brows together. "Adam?"

"I think so. I found it on the porch yesterday. I think he has a crush on me."

Brad grunted.

"I don't want to hurt his feelings, but I've got to let him know I'm not interested in him in *that* way."

"Want me to talk to him?"

"No, I can handle it. So what's new with you?"

"Same old, same old. Harri stopped by today."

"Uh-oh. Is that why you're here?"

"She's worried about you. You know how she gets when she thinks she's had a sign."

"You don't put much stock in her psychic powers."

"Nope. Doesn't matter though. She believes enough for both of us."

Grace twirled the glass, studying the light shining through the ice cubes.

"So here I am. Want to tell me what's bothering you? And don't say, *nothing*. I know you well enough to read that look on your face."

What could she tell him? That she didn't want to have a relationship with Tyler and he felt the same, yet she was upset about it? It even puzzled her why she felt hurt over his lack of attention today.

Grace met his concerned gaze. "I can't hide anything from you two. You probably know what I'm buying you for your birthday."

Brad's face lit with mirth. "I don't think Harri will give away that secret. But, don't change the subject. What's bothering you, hon?"

Who better to confide in than her best friend? She exhaled a long exasperated breath. "It's Tyler, and it's all your fault."

"Mine?"

"You told him I was looking for a job."

"So? Now you have one. What's wrong with that?"

"So, maybe I think he's...attractive."

Brad's grin grew larger. "Why's that a problem, darlin?"

Grace groaned. "Brad, come on. He's my boss. Look what happened with Connor."

Brad squeezed her hand. "Tyler's not Connor. He's a

fine young man with a sense of honor. You can't compare the two."

"Maybe not, but he's my boss. I don't need the complications."

"Is that what's bothering you or is it that headline in the paper?"

"You saw that, too?" She grimaced. "No. That's not bothering me. I find it amusing, though I can't figure out why Connor wants to keep our break-up a secret. It's not like he's planning on telling them why. He could blame it on me and get their sympathy. I don't know why he's so worried."

"Maybe he knows they'll take your side. After all, the press loves you. I don't think they really give a damn about Connor. He doesn't stand a chance of winning the election."

She frowned. "Why not? He's the perfect politician. He lies smoothly with a cool smile."

Brad made a scoffing noise. "That's probably true, but everyone can see right through his fancy words to the self-serving shell he really is."

"You don't have a very high opinion of him."

"Nope. And not just because he hurt you."

"He didn't really hurt me, Brad. Only my pride. I'm as much at fault as Connor." She grinned remembering what happened yesterday. "I did get even though."

"Yeah?"

She stood and leaned against the counter.

"Connor showed up here yesterday offering to have a discreet affair with me."

"What?" Brad jumped from his chair. Red suffused his face.

"Don't get your blood pressure up. Tiffany chased him off."

"Tiffany," he sputtered. "That mutt wouldn't hurt a flea."

"You should have seen him trying to fold himself into that little sports car while I threatened to let my 'trained-to-kill' guard dog loose."

"Trained-to-kill?" He slapped his leg, and belly laughed. Tiffany squirmed over to lean against him. He patted her head. "Good girl." He looked up at Grace with a huge smile. "Honey, I'd have paid to see that."

Grace chuckled. "It was funny. She took off after him like she meant to chomp off his leg, but what she did was much better."

Brad looked at her questioningly.

"She scratched his precious car." Grace dissolved in laughter.

Brad guffawed.

When he caught his breath he said, "Serves him right. If I'd been here, I might have put a bullet hole through the fender."

"Well, he is an attorney. I'll probably get a bill for damaging his property."

"I don't think so. He was on your property and he'd have to explain why. Wouldn't the press love that story?"

They shared another laugh.

"I'd better head for home and call Harri. She's probably biting her long purple fingernails to the nub. Now you stop worrying about Tyler being your boss. And don't put him in the same class as Connor. Give him a chance."

"A chance for what? He'd run like a gazelle if he knew the truth about me."

Brad kissed her forehead. "I think you're wrong. There's one way to find out, you know."

"It doesn't matter. He's not looking for a relationship and neither am I. It's just that he has this way of making a woman feel...special, and I needed that after Connor's put-down. It'll pass."

"How about me taking my two favorite women out for dinner tomorrow night? Maybe Harri can relieve your mind about Tyler." He wiggled his finger in front of her face as he did frequently. "I'm still not convinced that his being your boss is an issue."

Grace hugged him. "As it happens, I am free tomorrow night. You're impossible, but I still love you."

"And I'm grateful, darlin'. See you tomorrow."

Grace held open the door while Brad slipped out. "Thanks, Brad."

"You bet."

Then he was swallowed up in the dark, his flashlight jumping through the trees as he made his way back home.

****

The next morning, Adam caught up with her as she walked to work. "Hi, Adam." She waved, hoping he wouldn't expect her to stop and talk.

"Hi, Grace. I hear you're working at the clinic now."

"Yep. Isn't that great? Now I can walk to work. In fact, that's where I'm heading now. Don't want to be late."

He hurried to her side, keeping step with her. "Tyler isn't there. Had an emergency call. Lainey Miller's dog got hit by a car."

"Oh, no! How awful." A shiver ran down her spine. She could imagine how terrible it would be if something like that happened to Tiffany. She subconsciously stroked her dog's head.

Tiffany studied Adam without growling.

"You never know what'll happen if you don't keep an eye on your pets. When they run wild, bad things can happen."

An icy hand reached out to squeeze her heart. Adam's statement sounded like a threat.

Then he turned and walked away with a mumbled, "See ya, Grace."

"Yeah, see ya," she whispered.

She continued on toward the clinic, trying to forget about Adam. Tyler had given her a key, so she let herself in and checked the appointment book. While she was slipping into her lab coat, Tyler came in through the back.

"I thought you weren't here. Adam said—"

"Yeah. I had to take care of an injured dog. Ms. Miller's Dalmatian got loose and a car hit him. Nothing serious, just bruised him up a bit, thank God. He'll be fine in a few days."

Tyler squeezed her shoulder as he passed and Grace felt the tingle clear to her toes.

"Thanks for opening up, Grace."

"You're welcome. That's part of the job."

He smiled, a tired heavy-looking smile that did little to erase the grooves between his brows.

"Grace, I—"

Whatever he'd been about to say was interrupted by the clanging bell announcing their first patient.

Grace kept herself busy for the next three hours, periodically removing Muffin from her chair. Tiffany had stubbornly refused to stay in the clinic, and it made Grace nervous. She had never worried about Tiffany before, but Adam's words taunted her. He clearly didn't like her dog, but would he hurt her? She'd always thought of Adam as shy and kind of wimpy. She could imagine him saying: "Life is like a box of choc-o-lates." His attitude recently didn't fall into character, which made it even harder for her to approach him about the rose.

"Is that the last one?"

Grace jumped and turned startled eyes to Tyler. "I'm sorry. I didn't know you were standing there."

"A penny for your thoughts."

She shrugged.

A teasing light fired his eyes. "Were you thinking about me?"

There went the strange feeling in her stomach again. He stood close enough for her to reach out and push that lock of hair from his forehead. If not for the look in his eyes, she might have followed through with the action.

She tried for a neutral expression. "Why would I think about you? I think you have an over inflated ego."

"Who, me?" He looked properly offended.

She had to laugh despite her better intentions.

"Actually, I was worrying about Tiffany," Grace said.

Tyler leaned against the counter. "Why? She's not

going to run down to the main highway like Ms. Miller's dog, if that's what you're worried about. That was a freak accident." He reached out a hand and twirled one of her curls around his finger. "She's a smart dog."

His hands continued to caress her hair, setting her body on fire. She wanted to press her cheek against his hand, wanted him to pull her into his arms like he had—

He pulled his hand away and she felt the connection break. "So...last patient?" Tyler straightened and stuck his hands in the pockets of his white coat.

"Um," Grace looked at the appointment book though she knew the answer. "Yes, last one until two."

"Good. I'm hungry. Care to join me for a sandwich?"

Lord, she didn't want a sandwich, she wanted to be back in Tyler's arms with his tongue doing that erotic dance with hers.

"No thanks. I've got some things to take care of at home."

Was that disappointment crossing his face?

"Grace, you can't deny there's an attraction between us."

She paused with one arm in and one arm out of the lab coat. Her gaze locked on his.

"I haven't slept since Thursday night," he continued. "I keep thinking about that kiss, about how you felt in my arms, about the way your hair glows in the moonlight. I know I promised, but..."

He stepped closer and removed her lab coat, tossing it to the chair. He placed his hands on her shoulders and began to massage them. Her eyes closed, and she lost herself in his touch.

His fingers slid higher, up the side of her neck, threading together and cradling her head. She opened her eyes.

His nostrils flared and she breathed in his unique scent of citrus and animals. Mesmerized, she watched his head tilt, his lips part. A pulse throbbed in her neck rushing heat through her body.

"Grace." Her name was a moan on his lips...his tempting lips that moved closer.

Legs touched legs. She leaned into him, breasts brushing his chest, tingling, puckering, and begging for his touch.

The doorbell clanged.

Grace jumped back, startled. She heard Tyler's muffled curse followed by Adam's voice.

"How's Lainey's dog, Tyler?" Adam came to an abrupt stop. His gaze raked over them, narrowing when it met Grace's flaming cheeks.

Tyler answered, "He'll be fine. Just some bruises."

Grace busied herself clearing the reception desk.

"We're closing for lunch. Is there something I can do for you, Adam?" Tyler asked.

When she dared to look up, Adam's face burned an angry red. He opened the door. "No." The bell clanged as the door slammed shut behind him.

****

Kissing. Adam couldn't believe what he'd seen. She wouldn't have dinner with him, but she'd let that dog doctor paw her. Worst of all, she seemed to like it.

Adam stomped up the path, putting as much distance between the clinic and himself as possible. He'd had such plans for Grace. It had been years since a woman made him feel the things he did when he was near her. He wanted to protect her, shower her with nice things, *love* her.

Adam struck his fist against his leg. Then he hit it again, harder, relishing the pain that helped ease the gnawing agony of his broken heart.

He came to a stop and stared at the house his parents had lived in when he was born—Grace's house now. Another pain twisted inside. He'd sold the house to her hoping that one day he'd own it again after they were married. Their children would live in it and carry on the tradition.

Adam needed an heir, someone to take on the burden

of Foxfire when he died. It was a burden he'd carried alone for far too long. And he wasn't getting any younger. He'd waited too long for Lainey to change her mind. He still felt a pang of hurt when he thought of her and how he'd destroyed their relationship.

He straightened his shoulders. Maybe he'd misunderstood what he'd seen in the clinic. They might have been sharing a hug between friends. He hadn't *really* seen them kissing. Adam forced his gaze away from the house and he headed home to make plans.

A low growl stopped him. Grace's dog raised her head from the back porch, lifting her canine lips to show sharp, pointed teeth. Warning him.

Adam continued on his way. He'd have to do something about that dog. Maybe he'd get lucky and she'd run onto the highway and get killed. He'd console Grace by buying her a little lap dog, one of those furry non-threatening dust mops.

Grace really should watch her dog closer. One never knew what dangers lurked in these woods.

Chapter Seven

Damn his luck. Max threw some bills on the table and weaved his way through the restaurant toward the bank of telephones. He stood in the shadows pretending to make a call and watched as the hostess escorted Grace and her two crotchety friends to a table much too near where he'd been sitting.

Under the overhead glow of soft lighting, Grace's hair shone like the fur on a young vixen. Soon, he'd be running his fingers through it, letting the curls wrap him with molten fire. His hands would play her like a violin making sweet music. It had been too long since he'd had her in his bed. And he would have her one more time before he killed her.

****

"I have the strangest feeling that someone's watching us." Grace pulled her chair in closer to the table. She'd had a prickling feeling at the back of her neck from the moment they'd entered the restaurant.

"Darlin', everyone's looking," Brad said. "They're all wondering how I rate two gorgeous women."

Grace grinned and gazed across the table at Harri, dressed as usual in outrageous clashing colors. Her oversized pink earrings emphasized her double chin and her vivid blue tunic top draped softly over red and yellow striped slacks. Of course people were looking at them, but that wasn't what bothered Grace.

"So you feel it, too?" Harri narrowed her eyes.

Grace nodded.

Harri slipped her glasses onto her nose and accepted the menu from their waiter. Immediately, he recited the specials of the night, took their drink order and left.

Harri nodded toward the entrance. "See that man over there?"

Grace craned her neck and caught a glimpse of a dark-haired man in a business suit pushing his way outside. Something about him seemed vaguely familiar. "Who is that?"

"No idea, but did you see his dark aura?"

"I didn't see anything. How do you do that anyway?" She leaned across the table. "Can you teach me?"

"You just have to focus, dear. I'll be glad to work with you."

"Harri, don't start that nonsense. This is a celebration dinner." Brad turned to Grace with an apologetic grin.

"But I want to learn," Grace protested. "It's fascinating."

"Don't encourage her." He glanced at his menu. "What are you going to order, Harri?"

Grace studied the menu, wondering if the man Harri mentioned had been the one giving her the uneasy vibes, for she no longer felt them. She couldn't shake the idea that she knew him.

"I'm going to have the beef tips and noodles," Harri said.

The waiter returned and Brad placed his and Harri's orders. "What are you having, darlin'?"

Grace pushed the man's image out of her mind and gave her order to the waiter.

"Brad tells me you're falling in love with the vet," Harri said.

Grace had just taken a drink of water. She coughed and spewed water, grabbing quickly for her napkin.

"Now, Harri, that's not what I said," Brad challenged.

Harri waved a hand to quiet him. "Doesn't matter what you said. The truth is plain as day. I can see it in her—"

Brad scraped his chair back. "Excuse me." He slapped his napkin on the table. "I've got to visit the men's room." He glared at Harri. "Sometimes you really tick me off, Harriet."

Harri flipped a hand as if to say good riddance. "Men. They just don't understand these things." Harri stared intently into Grace's eyes. "Tell me what's going on."

Grace grabbed a napkin and dabbed at her mouth. "Not much. Just...well, we kissed. That's all."

"Is he a good kisser?"

Grace leaned forward conspiratorially. "The best."

"Um hum. So what are you going to do about it."

"Nothing! I told him to forget about it and he has."

"Um hum. That's what's really bothering you, isn't it?"

"He's my boss!"

"So what?"

"You know what happened with Connor."

"Connor is a lying, cheating fraud. Tyler..." She patted her lips with her forefinger and stared beyond Grace's shoulder. A moment later she looked back at Grace. "He's definitely got some issues. Like I said, there's something a little off in his aura, but I don't think he's anything like Connor."

From her peripheral vision, Grace saw a figure moving toward them.

"Hi, Grace. Harri."

Both women looked up at Adam, who stood twisting his hands and looking very out of place in a pin-striped suit, white starched shirt and bow-tie. His dark hair had been combed neatly back. Without the ever-present ball cap, Grace might not have recognized him if he hadn't spoken.

Grace stifled a groan. "Adam. What a surprise." Suddenly she wished they'd gone to Knoxville instead of choosing the only restaurant in Foxfire.

Harri harrumphed.

At that moment, Brad returned to the table. He held out a hand to Adam. "Hey, fancy meeting you here. Looks like we all had the same idea tonight." He sat and indicated the empty chair.

"Care to join us?"

Grace kicked his shin. The last thing she needed was to spend the evening with weird Adam.

Brad grimaced and pulled his brows down into a puzzled frown.

Adam flicked a glance at Grace, then shook his head. "No, I already ate. Just stopped to say hi." He waved a hand toward the front of the restaurant. A red flush crept up his neck. "Got a date."

They all turned to look. "Why don't you bring her over and introduce us."

"Uh, we're kind of in a hurry. Maybe some other time. Well..." He nodded at Grace. "Nice seeing you."

Grace felt a burden lift from her shoulders as she watched him stride away. If Adam was dating someone else, she didn't have to worry about hurting his feelings any longer.

Dinner passed uneventfully. Brad dropped Harri off, then drove toward Grace's house. He passed the animal clinic and Grace noticed Tyler's living quarters were dark. Where could he be? Nine p.m. seemed too early for him to be asleep.

Brad began to turn onto her drive. "Don't bother dropping me off. Just go to your house, Brad. I can walk from there. Tiffany will be waiting there for us."

Brad did as she asked. And as predicted, Tiffany ran to the car once it stopped.

"Thanks, Brad. I had a great time."

He hugged her. "You're welcome, darlin'. Me, too. And don't worry your pretty little head about Tyler. Things will work out. Just don't let the past get in the way of the future."

"Easier said than done."

"Just be open to possibilities. That's all I'm suggesting."

Grace pecked him on the cheek. "I'll try."

Would her past always haunt her? She'd made a bad

choice. Everyone made mistakes. She wasn't the only person to want more than life handed her. Could she learn to trust again? Forgive and forget?

Her troubled thoughts somersaulted through her mind as she strolled along the moonlit path in the woods. Stars twinkled and in the distance she spotted the greenish glow of foxfire. Halting, captured in the magical moment, she held her breath. No matter how many times she glimpsed the phenomenon, it continued to weave a spell. She blinked several times, but the light continued to glow. Could it be a sign?

Her spirits lifted as she continued along the path. Tiffany growled low in her throat and then dashed ahead. Grace heard the telltale rattle of the trashcan lid. She sprinted into the front yard, but Tiffany's bark echoed through the trees on the other side of the house. She called but the dog ignored her. Stupid raccoons. Shaking her head, Grace headed for the front door with her key in hand.

She sighed when she spied another rose on the doormat. She reached for the stem, felt a stab of pain and withdrew her hand. She stared at the bubble of blood that surfaced. She sucked at it. Pinching the stem between the long thorns, she lifted the rose to sniff its heady fragrance. A note card hung from a string tied beneath the bud.

Watch out for the thorns.

Weird. Just like Adam. She would have to talk to him after all. He had to stop leaving these floral gifts.

Grace walked into her darkened house, oblivious to the man watching her from the shadow of the woods.

****

Tyler roused himself from a light sleep and checked the caller ID. When he saw the number flashing, he ran a hand through his sleep-tousled hair. He'd been expecting to hear from Jake, but with only a couple hours sleep, he was in no mood to talk to him.

"Jake. What's up?" He yawned and scratched his

chest. Last night he'd kept watch on Grace's house until the sky began to lighten, then he'd crawled into bed only to toss and turn and think of her.

Jake rumbled a laugh, pulling him back to attention. "Sorry about waking you up, man, but I've got news. We caught up with Ted Powell. Unfortunately he had a bullet hole in his head."

Tyler whistled.

"So that leaves Grace Wilkins. Maybe it's time to put her in a safe house."

"No. I'll keep her safe."

"This is getting too dangerous, Tyler. Max is wreaking havoc and none of us has even come close to catching him. Any signs of him around there?"

"Negative. Maybe he won't show."

"Oh, he'll show. Have you told her yet?"

"I will. This just isn't a good time."

"What are you talking about?" Tyler held the phone away from his ear, but Jake's voice still came through loud and clear. "Someone wants to kill her! You have to tell her. Offer to put her in a safe house until we catch him. I'll send someone to back you up."

"No. I work better alone, you know that."

"You can't keep an eye on her twenty-four-seven."

"I'm handling it."

The pregnant pause gave him time to reconsider, but he didn't want any help. Hell, who was he kidding? If he could seduce Grace into his bed, he'd solve all his problems. He could keep her under guard and release the pent-up sexual frustration that built with every second he spent near her. He wouldn't let Max get his hands on her.

"This is big, Tyler. I don't have to tell you how big. He killed my sister."

The bitter pain of guilt twisted in Tyler's gut. "Yeah, I know, Jake. I loved her, too."

"I'm sorry, man. That wasn't fair. Look, I trust you. Tell Grace and let her make the decision. Then call me."

"Yeah. I'll call you."

He hung up the phone and rubbed the beard that peppered his chin.

Natalie's face flashed behind his eyes. He dropped his head to his hands, using his thumbs to massage the pain throbbing in his temples. Max might have pulled the trigger on the gun, but Tyler was ultimately responsible for Natalie's death. Like a tidal wave the memories crashed through his mind.

He owed Jake, and he'd pay him back by finding the man who'd killed Natalie. Then Tyler could move on with his life.

Regardless of the attraction he felt for Grace, his duty to bring Natalie's killer to justice came first. If he had to use Grace, he would. He couldn't afford to let his heart get in the way. Max Clayton wouldn't escape this time.

He buzzed the razor across his face and splashed on after-shave, dressed, and headed for Grace's house. He'd keep her under his thumb until Max made his move—his last move. He couldn't tell Grace the truth yet. She might bolt.

Tiffany met him on the path, her tail signaling a welcome.

She charged around the house once he reached Grace's yard. A few seconds later, Grace opened the screen door, her eyes widening in surprise.

"Tyler. Is something wrong? An emergency?"

Tiffany bounded out as if she hadn't seen him just moments ago.

"Not unless you call a case of spring fever an emergency. Would you like to walk to Hannah Falls with me? We could take a lunch and make a day of it."

He saw the hesitation in her eyes."I've heard it's a beautiful hike, and Brad told me you could be bribed with food."

"He did, huh? Whose job would it be to pack the lunch?"

He grinned. In the morning sun, the light caught the

gold highlights in her red hair, making her eyes look like a cerulean sea. She squinted at him, one eye nearly closing while she waited for his answer.

"Mine. Come on. Are you game?"

She glanced at her wristwatch. "Why not? Give me twenty minutes?"

"Deal."

****

Grace loaded a small backpack with bottled water. Before closing it she added a small plastic dish for Tiffany. With the temperature already climbing, water would be essential.

Tyler met her on the path, and Tiffany loped to his side, wriggling for attention. Grace's heart triggered a warning. No man should look so enticing in a t-shirt and jeans. Just one glance at those broad shoulders and muscled chest made her want to wriggle for attention, too.

"It's a great day for a hike," she said.

Tyler looked up at the clear blue sky. "Perfect."

They walked in companionable silence, the only cadence their muffled footsteps. Hannah Falls, named after Adam's great-great grandmother, drew visitors during all seasons. In winter, snowfall draped the ledges with crystalline diamonds, creating a breathtaking picture that begged for a camera. Grace made at least one trek in the winter, but summer's full sun brought life to a multi-tiered collage of plants and trees, making it her favorite season for the hike. When they arrived, Tyler spread a blanket on the ground, while Tiffany ran off to do whatever dogs do. The water cascaded softly over the rocks falling down to a narrow waterway leading to the Little Pigeon River. The sound brought a sense of peace.

Tyler pulled two thick sandwiches from the backpack and handed one to Grace. She poured a bottle of water into Tiffany's bowl. Pulling two more bottles from her stash, she handed one to Tyler, then leaned against a tree to peruse the landscape. "I wish I could paint."

Tyler grinned. "I've seen local artist paintings of the

Smoky Mountains, but none of Hannah Falls. It's even better than I imagined."

"That's because we protect our privacy."

"Interesting."

She waited a few moments, then asked, "Can I talk to you about something?"

He paused from unwrapping his sandwich, his gaze curious. "Sure. You're not going to tell me you're quitting, I hope."

She wanted to reach out and massage away the frown lines appearing in his forehead. "Of course not. I love the job."

"That's good. So what do you want to talk about?"

"You're a man."

"Last time I checked."

"I'm serious. I need your advice on how to deal with Adam."

"Adam?"

"I think he's got a crush on me. I found a rose on my porch last night."

"From Adam?"

"Yes, and it's not the first one he's left."

Tyler chewed his sandwich, his brow furrowed in concentration. "Why wouldn't he just give it to you instead of leaving it on your porch?"

"I don't know...he's strange. I think he likes me. You know, romantically. He asked me to have dinner with him and I turned him down. Then he started leaving roses on my doorstep."

"I see."

"I don't want to hurt his feelings, but besides being too old for me, he's not my type. It's beginning to creep me out."

"Have you talked to him about it?"

"No. That's the problem. I'm not sure how to do it. Don't get me wrong. Adam's not a bad sort. His family's been part of Foxfire forever. These falls were named after his great-great grandmother, did you know that?"

Tyler shook his head.

"I guess Adam's grandfather felt he owned not only most of the land around here, but also the people. He liked to keep an eye on everything. From what Brad says, you couldn't tell him anything he didn't already know. But when Jenny, that's Brad's wife, got sick, he stopped by every day to visit. Brad says he always made her smile."

"I didn't know Brad was married."

"Jenny died from cancer shortly before their fifth anniversary," she said.

"So Brad's been single ever since?"

She nodded. "I keep hoping he and Harri will get married, but he says he's too old." She laughed. "Imagine that. Brad seems so young and vital to me. I never think of him as old."

Tyler gave her a smile. "I know what you mean. He reminds me a lot of my dad."

"Tell me about your dad," she said, crossing her ankles.

"I'd rather hear about you. Tell me more about your life in...where was it? Missouri?"

She reached for her bottle of water. Since he had lived in Ohio, she couldn't very well tell him she also grew up there. "What do you want to know?"

"Whatever you feel like sharing."

She took a drink, wiped her mouth, and gazed at the waterfall. She wanted to trust Tyler, but she couldn't tell him the entire truth...not yet. If she talked about events without stating where they happened, it would be omission, not really telling a lie. She'd learned long ago that lying only led to trouble, and she had enough of that in her life already. She crossed her legs and leaned her arms across them. Her fingers plucked a blade of grass.

"I don't remember much about my dad. He left us before I started school. Mom wasn't the same after that. There were times when she seemed like any normal mother, and others when she became someone else." She shrugged. "Maybe she'd always been that way. Maybe that's why my dad took off."

"What do you mean?" His gaze pierced her with a burning intensity.

"She had...spells. I called them dark times. When she regressed into a dark time, nothing I did pleased her. As I grew older, I learned to stay away when she was like that."

"She hurt you?"

"Not physically."

They sat quietly for a few moments. Tyler was the first to break the silence.

"I'm sorry. You don't have to talk about it."

"It's all right. I stayed with her until she died."

Tyler traced a finger down her cheek. "I'm sorry."

"Don't be. She's happier now."

He lifted her chin. They stared into each other's eyes. Then he tilted his head and angled his lips over hers.

She knew she shouldn't kiss him, but her arms wrapped around his neck, pulling him closer. His tongue teased her. She opened her mouth, letting his tongue simulate what her body desired.

His lips were soft, his arms hard.

He eased her down to the blanket, his body covering hers. She felt the warm sun against her skin as he lifted the hem of her shirt. Goose bumps raised a trail everywhere his fingers touched.

Her breasts thrust tightly against her constraining bra. His thumb brushed the fullness, then his hand closed over her and she arched into his caress.

Their tongues tangled and she pushed against his pulsing erection. She wanted him, needed him.

He kissed a path down her neck. "Grace, I want to make love to you."

She gazed into his passion-glazed eyes. "I need you, too." She tugged at his shirt, pulled it loose, and reached for the zipper of his jeans.

Tiffany barked near by, then her bark turned to a

deep growl. Grace moaned, her hand resting against the bulge in Tyler's pants. What crappy timing.

Tyler growled, sounding much like Tiffany. "I'm going to muzzle your dog."

Tiffany's barks grew farther away as she gave chase to something.

"Probably a rabbit or a raccoon," Grace said. She laughed.

He reached for her again. "Now where were we?"

She pushed against his chest. "We can't. Not here."

"Bad timing, huh?"

"No, bad environment."

Tiffany came racing back and began to lap the water in her bowl.

Grace tucked her shirt into her jeans, and smiled at Tyler's heated gaze. Self-consciously, she tucked her hair behind her ears. She'd almost made the mistake of sleeping with her boss. Again. Would she never learn? First falling for a man like Max, just because he pretended to care for her, then Connor. Oh, sure she'd known Connor didn't love her, but she'd hoped time would make a difference. But Tyler? She knew better than to get her hopes up with a man like him. He'd expect complete honesty and he'd want someone untarnished, not a woman like her. If he learned the truth, he'd want nothing more to do with her.

Tiffany looked up, water dribbling from her jowls. Her ears pricked and a low rumbling growl rose from her chest. She raced into the thick foliage, baring her teeth.

Tyler sprang to his feet. "Grace, stay down."

"Why?"

"I think someone's out there."

Grace stood, ignoring his request. "I'll bet Adam followed us," she said.

"Wait here." He slipped into the woods, following Tiffany's snarls.

Grace began to gather their picnic supplies. So much for romance. Who needed it anyway?

Tyler soon returned shaking his head. "Nothing. She's snorting in the leaves now. You're right. It was probably an animal." He came to her and wrapped his hands around her waist pulling her to him. "I wish you'd change your mind."

"About what?"

"About this." With that he captured her lips with his bringing her back to the boiling point. His hands moved sensuously upward curving under her breasts. He angled his head and kissed the sensitive spot on her neck, just below her ear. "You're so beautiful," he whispered.

Grace forced her thoughts to where they were and who they were. She couldn't do this. Not until she told him the truth. If he still wanted her afterward, then and only then could she open herself to the possibility of a relationship. She pushed against his chest. "No." He raised his head and looked into her eyes. Did her eyes contain the same look of passion that his did? "Please."

He dropped his hands and stepped back. "What's wrong, Grace?"

She took a deep breath. "I just need some time. Things are moving too fast and I'm not ready."

He ran a hand through his hair. "You're right. We need to take it slower." A grin tugged at his lips and the teasing light was back in his eyes. "I like slow." He leaned down and picked up the remains of their picnic, then took her hand. "Come on. Let's take a nice slow walk back."

"Wait." She stooped and picked up an egg shaped rock.

"What's that for?"

She gave him a huge smile. "I'm not planning to use it on you, if that's what you're worried about. This is a perfect rock for painting."

"Painting?"

She nodded. "I'll show you sometime."

Tiffany ran back with a satisfied grin on her face.

"So you chased off our visitor, huh?" Grace asked. She knew Tiffany wouldn't have growled if she'd only been chasing an animal. Intuition told her Adam had been spying on them, and it wouldn't be the last time unless Grace confronted him. She wondered if he'd been lying about having a date last night. There was something about Adam that made her want to lock her doors and bar her windows.

When they reached Grace's house, Tyler headed on to the clinic and Grace went to Brad's.

She and Brad sat on the porch and she told him about finding the rose and the note.

"I'm not sure how to handle it," Grace confessed. "If you could talk to him, I'd be grateful."

"I'll do that. Strange note he left though. Doesn't sound like something Adam would do. In fact, the whole rose thing sounds out of character for him."

Grace nodded. "He's been different lately, though. Ever since he asked me out. But it seems strange that he had a date and still left a rose, don't you think?"

He patted her knee. "I'll have a talk with him and see what I can do."

"Thanks, Brad."

"So you and Tyler went to Hannah Falls?"

"Yes." She grinned. "As if you didn't know about it ahead of time. Tyler told me you said I could be bribed with food."

Brad cackled. "You enjoyed it, didn't you?"

"It was...nice." She could feel her cheeks warming. It was a whole lot better than nice, but she wasn't about to share that with Brad. "There's been enough rain to make the waterfall heavy. You and I will have to go soon."

"Maybe."

"What do you mean, maybe? We always go there several times a year."

He grinned. "Well, now you have Tyler. You young ones should go and leave an old codger like me to rock on my porch."

"Stop. You're not old, and you're my best friend. Of course we'll go. Tyler's just my boss."

"Mmm-hmm. If you say so."

Grace knew Brad was teasing her, so she changed the subject. "Who do you think Adam had a date with last night?"

"Beats me. You'd think he'd bring her to our table, but Adam is kind of private. Too bad his folks left him so well off. He needs to spend more time around people, not stay holed up in that house all the time. No wonder he's so hard to communicate with."

"Hasn't he ever worked?"

"As far as I know, he's never worked a day in his life, except for volunteering at the library."

"He doesn't seem like a man who reads much."

Brad shrugged. "You'd be surprised. Adam might not sound educated, but he's a smart man."

"Interesting." She kissed Brad's cheek. "Thanks for the chat. If you talk to Harri, tell her I'll give her a call soon."

****

Tyler went through the motions of fixing dinner and cleaning up, but his mind swirled with images of Grace and Natalie. He'd come to Foxfire with only one goal. To catch the bastard who killed his wife. He'd thought the key to success was through Grace, but he'd been wrong. Grace didn't have a clue that Max had begun a killing spree, nor that her life was in danger. Max had used Grace as ruthlessly as he had Natalie. Thankfully Grace escaped his clutches. She wasn't at all what Tyler had expected. Despite what she endured in the past, she'd forged a new life and she looked at each day with the optimism he longed to have. How had she found peace? How did she let go and move forward?

He walked out onto the deck and gazed through the trees toward her house. He could see a small glimmer of light. What was she doing now? Would she be preparing for bed? He wondered if she wore cotton shirts or black silk lingerie...or...nothing at all when she crawled between the sheets of her bed.

With an oath, he went inside and locked the door.

Chapter Eight

Brad set out a plate of Harri's oatmeal cookies. When he'd called, Adam didn't question why, just said he'd be right down. It made Brad feel a bit guilty for spending so much time with Tyler over the past weeks. He hadn't meant to ignore Adam.

When Grace asked Brad to question Adam about the roses, he assured her he would. Maybe he shouldn't use their friendship this way, but Brad wanted to prevent Grace from confronting Adam. If anyone could salvage the situation, Brad was the one to do it.

When Adam knocked, Brad waved him in. "Make yourself at home."

Adam pulled out a chair and sat down. "Sorry I couldn't join you for dinner last night."

"Had a date, huh?"

"Yeah."

"Anybody I know, or would you rather not tell?" Brad handed a mug to Adam and pushed a plate, mounded with cookies, across the table. "Have one of Harri's cookies. Made fresh yesterday."

Adam bit into one and leaned back against the chair. One arm rested on the table. He spoke around the food he continued to chew. "It was Lainey." He dipped the cookie into the coffee and stuffed it into his mouth. "These 'er good."

"I'll let Harri know." Brad sipped his coffee. "Lainey, huh? You two getting back together?"

"We're just friends, I guess."

Brad saw his opening. "Nothin' wrong with having friends of the opposite sex. Kind of like me and Grace." He watched Adam's face and saw a brief flicker of something

86

unreadable cross his features.

Adam nodded. "You're lucky she sees you as a friend."

"Grace is your friend, too, Adam."

"Nah. I don't think she likes me much."

"Why not?" Brad helped himself to a cookie.

Adam pushed back his hat and scratched his head.

"I asked her to dinner and she turned me down. And her dog hates me."

"Tiffany? She likes everybody."

Adam shook his head. "Not me. I think she knows I'm scared of her."

"Thought you'd gotten over being afraid of dogs."

Adam's eyes opened wider. "I tried, but it didn't work. Dogs still scare the beejeezus out of me. Especially big dogs. Grace lets hers run loose all the time. That's not good. Look what happened to Lainey's dog the other day when that car hit it." He shook his head. "Grace should be more careful."

Adam gobbled another cookie. Crumbs floated on the top of his coffee, but he didn't seem bothered.

"Want another cup?" Brad asked.

"Sure." Adam pushed his mug toward Brad. "I've missed our visits. Figured you were too busy for your old friends."

"I've been busy, but I never forget my friends. As a matter of fact, I want to invite you to dinner next Sunday. I've already invited Harri and Grace. And Tyler. You could ask Lainey."

"Does Grace know you're inviting me?"

"Yes." He didn't think God would hold one fib against him. Especially since it was for a good cause.

Adam's face lit. "Really? And she wasn't upset?"

"Not upset, but she's a bit concerned about the roses you're leaving her."

"Roses? Me?"

His hand, wielding another cookie, stopped short of his mouth. His eyes seemed to double in size. Adam couldn't be that good an actor. He obviously knew nothing about it.

"I never gave her any flowers," he said.

Brad poured two fresh mugs of coffee and handed one to Adam. He took a sip before responding. "Hmmm. She thought it was you."

"What about Tyler? I saw the two of them kissing."

"Uh-uh. The first one was left the day Connor came to her house. You were there that day, weren't you?"

"What is this, the third degree?" Adam rose from the chair.

Brad patted his arm. "Sorry. I just wondered if he might have left it."

"That bum? Doubt if he'd do anything nice like that. He was real mean to Grace. I told her if he came back to let me know. I'd like to have a piece of him, I would." Adam stuffed the cookie in his mouth and sat down.

"Looks like we've got a mystery on our hands. Someone's been leaving those roses. She found another one after we got home from dinner last night."

Adam leaned both forearms on the table, putting his face closer to Brad's. He looked left and right as if expecting someone to overhear. "We ought to keep an eye on her house. Maybe we can catch the guy in the act. We don't want anything bad to happen to Grace."

Brad's scalp crawled. "What do you mean?"

Adam stopped chewing, mouth agape, showing more than Brad cared to see. "Are you kidding me? With all the murders?"

"In *Knoxville*. Not Foxfire. There's no one here who would hurt a soul." Or was there?

"Maybe so, but we have to be careful. Bad things happen even in safe communities, you know."

Brad wondered if Adam was telling the truth. Would he lie to a friend? If Adam wasn't the one leaving the flowers, who could it be?

****

Grace stood beside her living room window and

stared at Adam from behind the veil of curtains. She glanced nervously at her watch. She couldn't stall too much longer or she'd be late for work. Why was he waiting for her?

Steeling herself for the worst, Grace stepped outside and pulled the door shut behind her. Readjusting her purse strap over her shoulder she waved. "Hi, Adam."

He nodded. "I've been waiting for you."

Tiffany ran toward him and he backed away nervously.

"Tiffany, stop."

She did. She sat close to Adam's feet.

Surprised that she didn't growl, Grace wondered if she was wrong about Adam. Tiffany didn't seem upset to see him. Maybe Adam hadn't been the one who'd followed them to Hannah Falls.

"I think she's trying to make friends with you."

Adam held a trembling hand down and Tiffany sniffed.

"See? Go ahead and pet her." Would Tiffany be so passive if Adam was a threat? No way.

Adam stretched a hand out, but Tiffany moved away.

He snatched his hand to his chest, his eyes widening fearfully. "She don't like me." Adam's gaze met Grace's. "You really should keep her on a leash."

Out of the question. There were no restrictions in Foxfire. Besides, Tiffany was a free spirit. And regardless of Adam's fear, she knew her dog wouldn't hurt a soul. She bit back a sharp retort, knowing it would serve no purpose. "Did you need something, Adam?"

"I'll walk you to work," he said. "I want to talk to you about the roses."

Adam kept pace as they walked toward the clinic, while Tiffany raced ahead.

"Brad told me it wasn't you who left them."

"And that's the truth. But somebody did, that's for sure."

"Yes, *somebody* did." Grace still felt it was Adam.

"What about Tyler? You two seem to be pretty *friendly*."

There it was again, a spark of jealousy. "No. I was coming back from visiting the clinic the first time I found a rose. It wasn't there when I left the house. That was the day Connor stopped by. I'm sure you remember. *You* were there."

She tried, but couldn't keep the accusation from popping out.

Adam stopped walking. "And because of that, you think it was me?"

She shrugged, then grabbed for her falling purse strap. "I thought since you asked me out—"

"You turned me down, didn't you?" His voice rose. "Why would I leave flowers for a woman who won't even have dinner with me?"

She had to tell him the truth, make him understand once and for all that she wasn't interested in him romantically. "Adam, I don't want to hurt your feelings. I think of you as a friend, nothing more."

He stared straight ahead. "I only want to be your friend, Grace. I care about you, but not..." His face reddened. "I've got a girlfriend already."

She sighed with relief. "That's wonderful, Adam. I'm happy for you, and I'm sorry I misread your intentions. Forgive me?"

"No hard feelings between friends." He grinned at her.

"I've got to hurry so I'm not late for work." Grace began to walk away.

Adam kept in step until they came to the end of the path and turned to face her. "You be careful, Grace. You never know what kind of perverts there are in this world. Look at all the women who've been murdered right here under our noses."

Grace shuddered. "That happened in Knoxville, not here."

Adam's intense gaze pinned her. "Didn't you read the

paper this morning? They found another dead body." He pulled his cap lower. "In the woods behind the restaurant. No place is safe." Without a further word, he turned and strode away.

Behind the restaurant? A trace of fear set up residence. She hadn't read the paper this morning. If what Adam said was true, a total of five women had been killed now. She shivered.

All murdered with a knife. The woods suddenly seemed to have eyes. She ran the rest of the way to the clinic.

****

Tyler heard the door open and peered around the doorframe. His heart picked up cadence when he saw Grace. She rushed toward him.

"What's wrong?"

"Nothing."

She grabbed her lab coat from the hook.

"Something happened. You look like you've seen a ghost."

"No ghost. Just Adam."

He leaned against the desk.

"What did he do this time?"

"I swear everything he says sounds like a threat."

She shoved her arms into the lab coat.

"Whoa. Adam threatened you?"

Grace lifted her shoulders in a shrug. "I don't know. It seemed that way. He's a very strange person."

"What did he say?"

"It's nothing. I overreacted. He does that to me."

Before Tyler could question her further, the doorbell jangled, signaling their first patient for the day. Over the next few hours, Tyler and Grace were too busy for small talk. While grateful for the business, he longed for a break so he could learn more about her conversation with Adam.

After ushering out the last patient before the lunch break, Tyler leaned over the reception counter. "Lunch? I've got ham sandwiches with lettuce and mayo."

She looked up, her eyes growing a deeper blue. "I should—"

The telephone rang and Grace snatched it, muttering a fast "Foxfire Animal Clinic." Her face paled. "He's here. Please hold." She hit the hold button and looked up at Tyler. "It's Mr. Jacobson. His dog is really sick."

Tyler put the phone to his ear, and as he listened his heart sank. He assured Mr. Jacobson that he'd come right away, then handed the phone to Grace, asking her to get directions. He hurried to the back of the office.

A few minutes later, he returned with his medical bag. She held up a slip of paper. "Here you go."

"Grace, would you mind coming with me? I'm afraid I'll have to put his dog down. I could use your help."

She nodded, tears shimmering in her eyes. "Okay." She grabbed several tissues and stuffed them into her pocket.

"Would you navigate?" Tyler asked.

"Sure."

They climbed into his truck.

"I don't know if I can do this." Grace's voice broke.

Tyler reached for her hand and squeezed it. "This is going to be hard. I shouldn't have asked you to come." He glanced at her profile. She lifted her chin, a familiar gesture, and his heart did that crazy jig again.

"I'm fine."

He put the truck in gear and drove off, following her directions through the back roads. Soon they pulled into a gravel drive next to a small but well-kept house. A man opened the door and waited while they climbed from the truck. He leaned heavily on a cane, his hands crippled and withered from arthritis and age. His keen brown eyes peered at them from behind gold-framed glasses. "Thanks for coming, Doctor Sandford."

Tyler held out a hand. "Call me Tyler, Mr. Jacobson, and this is Grace Wilkins."

"Pleased to meet you. Spanky's in the bedroom."

He turned and walked away, surprisingly fast

despite his handicap.

Tyler knelt beside the large short-haired dog. Spanky looked as if he was part German Shepherd. The dog wagged his tail, but made no effort to rise.

"He's been that way all day. I tried to get him on his feet, but he just lays there. I gave him food and water, but he hasn't touched either one."

The haze over the dark eyes told Tyler the dog had impaired vision. His muzzle, which had once been dark, was now heavily peppered with white. Tyler did a quick examination. "Did he vomit or show any signs of distress?"

"He threw up this morning. I heard a noise and found him thrashing around like he was trying to get to his feet. Then he just flopped over on his side. What do you think's wrong?"

Tyler lifted his gaze to the old man. "I'm sorry, Mr. Jacobson. It looks like he had a stroke. I doubt he'll ever walk again." He paused, letting the information hang in the air. The dog should be put to sleep, but he didn't want to be the first to mention it.

The old man stared into the distance. "Call me Will. Short for William, after my dad." He shuffled to the bed and sat on the mattress. "You're thinking he should be put down, aren't you?"

Grace took a ragged breath. Tyler caught the sheen in her eyes, though she clearly struggled to maintain a calm façade. How could he have ever thought she had been part of Max's network? Everything she'd said at the trial was true. She hadn't known about Max's illegal affairs. If anything, Grace had been a victim, too. He took Grace's hand and gave it a gentle squeeze, then turned to Mr. Jacobson.

"I'm sorry, but I think it would be the humane thing at this point."

Will nodded.

"He's been my best friend for nearly sixteen years. My wife, Helen, got him for me before she passed on.

Guess it's time for him to be with her now."

Grace put her free arm around the old man's shoulder. "He was lucky to have such a wonderful home, Mr. Jacobson."

Tyler dreaded what he had to do. Putting an animal to sleep was the worst part of being a vet. Watching the owner's pain, the brief indecision, the guilt, and then the overpowering sorrow.

Will said, "It's his time. I just wish I could have gone first."

"Would you like to stay with him?" Tyler asked.

Will nodded.

"Do you have a sheet we can use?" Tyler asked. He glanced at Grace. She swallowed visibly.

Will removed a quilt from the foot of the bed and handed it to Tyler. "This do?"

Tyler nodded. "We're going to lift him to the bed next to you."

Unashamedly, tears streamed from Will's eyes. He removed his glasses and pulled a handkerchief from his back pocket. "Thank you."

Tyler maneuvered the heavy dog onto the blanket, receiving a friendly tongue kiss. He and Grace each took up the ends of the quilt and lifted the dog to the bed.

The sadness in Grace's eyes knifed through Tyler's heart. He wanted to pull her into his arms and tell her he could give the dog a magic pill to restore his health, but that was beyond his capabilities. At times like this, he questioned his choice of profession, but on the plus side, he spent most of his time healing and feeling he was contributing something positive to the world. In his dual occupation of agent, there was always another scumbag to take the place of the ones they caught. That's another reason he couldn't wait to turn in his gun.

Will placed his hand on Spanky's head. He talked softly about watching over Helen until he could join them.

Tyler filled a syringe, sucking up the liquid that would end the dog's life. Who was he to play God? His hands trembled. He looked into Spanky's eyes and swore he could see into his soul. The dog rolled his gaze up to his owner, then back to Tyler. Intelligence lived in that gaze...and acceptance...and forgiveness.

Will looked up, nodded, and Tyler inserted the needle.

He swallowed the lump in his throat, watching Will's hand guiding the dog toward peace. He felt the pain of Will's loss. Had Natalie known he loved her at the moment she took her last breath? Had he told her he loved her, let her know the depth of his feelings? He hadn't given her the one thing she asked for. More of himself. He'd wanted to, but somehow the job always pulled more of his time than he planned. He got caught up in the thrill of the chase and the glory of the capture, forgetting how much he'd always loved working with animals. He glanced back at Spanky. It was over. He'd taken a life. Tyler waited a few more minutes, then gently placed his stethoscope on the dog's chest.

He looked up at Will. "He's gone."

Will's tears streamed down his face as he continued to stroke his beloved friend.

Grace murmured, "I'm so sorry, Mr. Jacobson."

Will blew his nose loudly and stuffed the handkerchief in his back pocket. "He's with Helen now. He'll watch over her until it's my time."

"You should get another dog," Grace said.

Will shook his head. "I don't think so." He ran his hand down Spanky's side. He raised his head and looked at Tyler. "I'd like to bury him out back among the trees. That was his favorite spot."

Tyler started to protest, then remembered he wasn't in the city and no one would mind an animal being buried in the back yard. Besides, how could he say no? "I'll be glad to help," he offered.

"So would I," Grace said.

"Thank you. These arms aren't quite what they used to be."

****

The closer she came to home, the faster Grace ran. Watching Tyler bury Mr. Jacobson's dog was one of the hardest things Grace ever endured. She'd held back the tears until she'd escaped Tyler's presence. She'd even managed to console Mr. Jacobson without breaking down. Now all she wanted to do was hug her dog.

Grace ran across the yard, her face burning from the sun's heat. "Tiffany!"

She yelled louder, hurrying to the back porch where Tiffany liked to slumber. Tiffany raised her head, then slowly got to her feet, stretched her legs and neck, then shook herself. She barked a greeting, then loped to Grace's side, tail waving.

Grace threw her arms around the dog and squeezed so hard Tiffany gave a soft yelp.

"I'm sorry, girl." Grace cradled Tiffany's head between her hands and gazed into her soulful eyes. "I love you." She kissed the cold wet nose.

Tiffany squirmed free and ran a circled path in the yard. Her long fur drifted like silk in the wind, her ears perked, and her eyes danced with mischief.

Grace's smile pushed away the tears that earlier clogged her throat. What would she do without Tiffany? She'd fallen in love with the ball of fur from the moment she'd popped her head out of the box Brad had garnished with Christmas wrapping and ribbon. She couldn't bear to think of the day she'd have to say goodbye like poor Mr. Jacobson did today.

Her heart went out to the brave old man who'd lost his wife and now his furry companion. She wanted to do something to ease his pain. Maybe she and Tiffany could go and visit him from time to time. She could bake him some cookies or brownies, spend a few hours talking to him, letting him reminisce. Yes, definitely she'd make time to do that.

"Come on, Tiffany. Let's go visit Brad."

As usual, the dog bounded ahead, already knowing

their destination. Brad sat on the back porch, shucking a batch of corn. She sat next to him, grabbed an ear and pulled the husk and silk away from the golden yellow kernels.

"What's wrong, darlin'?"

She smiled into Brad's clear blue eyes. "I can't visit my best friend without something being wrong?"

"Sure you can." He set his rocker in motion. "I've got a fresh batch of ice cream in the freezer." He continued to work on the corn without looking directly at her.

Tiffany's ears lifted as if she understood.

Grace dropped the clean ear of corn in the pan. "I suppose I could eat a bowl."

Brad rose to his feet "Then let's have at it. I'll finish the corn later."

They followed an established ritual of Grace getting the bowls, while Brad retrieved the ice cream and began dipping it out. They sat across from each other and Grace took a bite before meeting Brad's gaze. He gave her a slight grin.

"We had to put Mr. Jacobson's dog down today."

His smile disappeared. "That's too bad. Will is a good man. Lost his wife not long ago, too. Must have been hard on him."

Grace swallowed the lump that rose in her throat. She would *not* cry. She nodded, keeping her eyes on her bowl.

"Must have been hard for you, too."

Again, Grace nodded without speaking.

"Course you could always check the Foxfire Animal Shelter. Bet they've got a lot of unwanted dogs." He scratched his chin. "Yep, that just might be a nice thing to do."

Why hadn't she thought of that? She'd ask Tyler tomorrow. He could help her pick out a perfect dog for Mr. Jacobson. It would be just the thing, no matter how Will had rejected the idea today. No animal could take the place of Spanky, but having a new dog to care for would give him something positive to focus on.

Grace jumped up and ran to Brad. She kissed his weathered cheek and hugged him tight. "You're a genius."

Brad chuckled. "You'd have thought of it yourself, hon."

"You think he'll accept a new dog?"

Brad patted her on the arm. "I'm sure. You might want to wait a spell though. Give him a few days to grieve for Spanky."

Grace attacked her ice cream with fervor. "Do you want to go to the shelter with me?"

Brad's eyes twinkled. "Three's a crowd, hon."

Had he read her mind? "What do you mean?" she asked trying to look confused.

He winked. "You and Tyler can take care of it." He laid his spoon beside his bowl. "How about you two coming to dinner tonight? I've got a dozen ears of corn out there on the porch. Harri's bringing the main course, though Lord only knows what that'll be."

Grace still felt kind of hollow inside. She didn't think she could keep up a happy front for a whole evening, especially with Tyler there to remind her of what they'd done today. All she wanted tonight was to soak in a hot tub and curl up with a good book with Tiffany for company.

"I think I'll take a rain check, but thanks for asking. I'm kind of washed out."

"Sure, hon, I understand."

She looked up at him. "Did you read the article in the paper about the body behind the restaurant?"

He clunked his spoon on the table. "Terrible. Just like the others, she was murdered somewhere else and her body was left there. What kind of evil person can do such a thing?"

She shivered. "It's scary. I mean this makes it personal, doesn't it? It's not like something happening far away. It's right here."

He reached over and patted her arm. "It didn't

happen here, honey."

"We don't know that. For all we know all those women could have been killed here and moved to Knoxville or other places afterward."

"Enough talk about it. I'm not into speculation. Besides, there's no one in Foxfire who would do such a thing. This is a quiet, safe community. We have a zero crime rate."

They finished their dessert in comfortable silence, then Grace took her leave.

She walked more slowly back toward her cabin. Rounding a bend in the path where she could no longer see Brad's house behind her, she felt a chill despite the heat of the day. She increased her pace. She felt certain someone was watching them, but Tiffany seemed unaffected. It had to be her imagination.

When she reached her house, she stopped in surprise.

Tyler rose from the front steps and dusted the back of his jeans.

"Hi," he said. "I didn't feel like being alone. Could I keep you company?"

"Great," Grace mumbled. She'd finally pushed the sadness far enough away that she no longer felt like crying, but seeing Tyler brought it all rushing back.

He shrugged his shoulders. "If you'd rather be alone—"

"No," she interjected. "It's fine. I mean, I *could* use some company."

Tiffany jumped up, resting her paws on Tyler's chest and licking his face.

"Down, Tiff," Grace ordered.

Tyler laughed, tilting his head away from the dog's tongue. "It's all right." He pushed Tiffany gently to all fours.

"Come on in," Grace invited, leading the way to the front door. She mentally ran through the items in her fridge, wondering if she should call Brad and take him up on his earlier offer.

"Are you hungry?" she asked.

"Not really." He looked around her sparse living room. "You know, I do like your house."

She grinned. "I don't entertain much. Tiffany doesn't require much in the way of furniture. We can sit in the kitchen if you want." She gestured toward the open doorway.

"No, I meant what I said. It's simple, but warm." He seated himself on the hearth and picked up a rock that had been painted into a sleeping kitten. He picked up several others, dogs, rabbits and turtles, examining them carefully. Finally, he smiled up at her and wrapped his arms around his knees. "You're very talented."

"Thanks."

Grace sat in the rocker.

Tiffany came out of the kitchen, her jowls dripping water. She walked to Tyler and leaned against him. He ruffled her fur and she dropped to the rug at his feet.

Grace felt awkward. What could they talk about to avoid the issue forefront in both their minds?

He met her gaze. "The first time I had to euthanize an animal, my dad was with me. Later we sat and talked about it. He helped me understand what I'd done was the humane thing." Tyler shook his head. "I still have a hard time dealing with it. No matter how prepared you are, it always hurts to see life fade away."

Grace swallowed. The lump kept rising in her throat. She wouldn't resort to tears in front of Tyler. She bit the inside of her mouth, a trick that always worked. She watched Tyler's fingers absently stroking Tiffany's ears.

"I suppose you get hardened to it," she said.

"Never."

Grace lifted her head and met his gaze. They stared into each other's eyes, and her stomach flipped. Her heart seemed to stop, then picked up speed, thumping erratically. "I...it was hard for me."

Tyler unfolded his arms and rose to his full height. "For me, too."

She had to force her gaze away, regain control. She'd let Tyler get past her protective shell again. She'd never allowed anyone but Brad to see her soft side.

"I was talking to Brad. He suggested getting Mr. Jacobson another dog."

Tyler moved closer. "That's a great idea."

****

Tyler watched the emotions cross her face. He'd known she'd be hurting. He'd spoken the truth when he said he never got over putting an animal to sleep. He wanted to take Grace in his arms and comfort her, and draw comfort *from* her, but he kept his distance, knowing she wasn't ready. Neither was he. He still had a job to do, and that job required him to stay focused on one thing. Catching a killer—a killer who wanted to murder Grace, and that scared the hell out of him.

She looked down at Tiffany, avoiding his gaze.

"Want to go for a walk?" he asked.

Grace shook her head.

"A drive?"

She shook her head again. Damn. He needed to find a way to break through the walls she'd put up. He told himself it was all to maintain his cover, but he knew better.

If he walked away now, she'd break down, have her cry and it would help. He should respect her right to do that and head back to his lonely apartment. But he didn't want to leave her alone. And it had more to do with his feelings than Grace's. With Grace, he'd begun to believe that he could move on with his life. The grief that had kept him awake night after night, month after month, year after year, had begun to heal. He felt the hard ice of his heart chipping away, bit by bit as he settled into his new life. He reached out and squeezed Grace's shoulder.

"The animal shelter is open until seven." The words popped out surprising him. He shouldn't let himself get personally involved, but what was happening between them had nothing to do with catching a killer.

Another chunk of ice melted when Grace lifted her gaze to his.

"Brad said we should wait a few days."

Tyler grinned. "We could pick out a dog and keep it at the clinic. That way I can make sure it has all the required shots and is in good health before we hand it over."

"You'd be willing to do that? Keep it at the clinic, I mean."

He placed a hand on his heart and gave her a look of feigned surprise. "How could you doubt me?"

Her eyes lit and a smile tilted her lips upward. God, she was beautiful when she smiled. She didn't need makeup or any artificial enhancements. Her beauty came from within.

"I'd love to go," she said.

"Let's do it."

"Let me grab my purse. I'm sure the shelter accepts donations."

Every male hormone came into play as he watched her walk down the hall, her hips swaying in subtle rhythm.

He called out, "We can stop for a bite to eat first. That is if you've gotten your appetite back."

She stuck her head around the doorway. "Brad invited us to dinner, but I told him I wasn't in the mood to be with anyone. I'll call him back and tell him I've changed my mind. That is...if you want to. Harri's going to bring the main course."

He didn't want to share Grace with anyone tonight. He preferred to think of the two of them in his bed sharing a glass of wine and a plate of strawberries. He hid his disappointment behind a smile. "Psychic casserole?"

She laughed and a moment later returned with a purse slung over her shoulder. "Whatever it is, it'll be scrumptious. Harri's a great cook."

"Sounds good."

She called Brad and told him she and Tyler would

share dinner with him and Harri after all. When she hung up, she said, "I'm ready. Let's go get that dog."

So was he. Ready to carry her off to bed. He concentrated on banking the fire she'd started in his loins. "I'll get the truck and pick you up."

"No need. I can walk down with you."

There went that smile again. He reached for her hand and she didn't protest. It felt right snuggled inside his.

Twenty minutes later, he held open the door while Grace entered the shelter's noisy reception area. Cats roamed freely in a large cage, bumping against the bars as they passed. One reminded him of Muffin. He still had no idea who the cat belonged to, but he wasn't complaining. He'd gotten used to her company.

An elderly woman with chipmunk cheeks and little round glasses riding on the end of her nose greeted them. She reminded him of Mrs. Claus. She led them to a room in the back. "What kind of dog are you looking for?" she asked.

Grace said, "A big one—"

"A mutt—" Tyler said in unison.

Tyler laughed. "We're looking for a big lovable mutt."

They perused the cages, stopping to pet and talk to each animal. Tyler knew it would be hard to choose. Grace kept moving back to a brown speckled mixed breed. The animal was less than a year old, and hadn't yet grown into its rather large paws. Tyler scratched behind the dog's ears and received a wet puppy kiss in return.

"We'll take this one," Tyler said. He looked for Grace's approval. She gave him her hundred megawatt smile in answer.

Decision made, Tyler filled out the paperwork and left a generous donation. Before leaving, he handed the woman his business card.

"Oh, my. You're the new veterinarian."

"That's me." He leaned down as if to share a secret. "I'm offering my services if you need a volunteer."

Her face lit with pleasure. "Oh, thank you, Doctor. I'll talk to the manager and he'll get in touch with you. You don't know how grateful we are. The shelter survives on donations alone. Sometimes it's difficult to come up with the money to pay for emergencies. We could offer you a small compensation."

He patted her hand. "I wouldn't dream of taking a penny."

"You're the answer to a prayer," she responded.

And so the wheels had been set in motion. Tyler would be staying in Foxfire when his assignment was finished. Looking down on Grace's shiny red curls, he decided his life had finally taken a turn. A turn for the better.

Chapter Nine

Three days later, Grace opened her mailbox and removed a large brown envelope. Her name and address had been printed in neat block letters, but there was no return address. She studied it for a moment, wondering who had sent it. It weighed next to nothing. What could it be?

Curiosity got the best of her and she pulled the strip to open the envelope. Peering inside she saw a silk ivory scarf.

"What in the world?" She pulled it out and a piece of paper fluttered to the ground. The scarf draped luxuriously across her arm. The silk shimmered in the morning sunlight. She ran her hand down the length, its simplistic beauty mesmerizing her. She loved the feel of silk. Her one vice was silk lingerie, though she kept that secret to herself.

Last night, Tyler had kissed her goodnight after walking her to the door. Could this be a present from him? He said that her skin looked and felt like silk. A rush of pleasure warmed her. No matter that she had fought against it, she was falling for Tyler. He made her feel beautiful, not outside, but inside where for so long she'd felt soiled.

She lifted the silk to her cheek, closed her eyes, and rubbed its smoothness against her face. Today they were taking the dog they'd adopted to Mr. Jacobson. They'd named him Shane. Her heart beat a little faster at the thought that soon she'd see Tyler. She placed the scarf around her neck and looped it, letting it drape across her chest. What did it matter that she was dressed in jeans and a cotton t-shirt? She'd wear it to show Tyler how pleased she was with his gift.

Tiffany sniffed at the paper that had fallen at Grace's feet.

Grace stooped and picked it up. The words scorched her vision. Printed in block letters was a name that made the bile rise in her throat. *Gracie Jo.* Only one person had called her that—the man she'd been hiding from for three years—Max Clayton. She read the note again. *Gracie Jo. I know you like silk. This is for you. A gift. Like old times. How did you like the roses? Weren't they pretty? Such a vivid shade of red. The color of fresh blood.*

"No!" She ripped the offending article from her neck and tossed it to the ground. Her hands trembled and she spun in circles, staring into the trees, wondering if he was watching. He'd found her. He'd found her. Oh, God, he'd found her.

She wanted to run back to the house, lock herself inside, and cower under the bed. She had thought she'd be safe here, but nowhere was safe. Not even Foxfire. And that meant...tears stung her eyes...no one was safe. Not Brad, nor Harri, nor Tiffany. And God forbid, not even Tyler.

Grace snatched up the horrid scarf. "Come on, Tiff." Holding her chin high, Grace led the way back to her house.

She had a job to do. She and Tyler were taking Shane to Mr. Jacobson today. Tonight she'd deal with the issue of Max. He was taunting her. He wanted her to cower, and she wouldn't allow him to have that control over her. She wouldn't run away. Not this time.

Tiffany seemed to sense Grace's fear and stayed close by her side as she walked behind the house, lifted the trash can lid and tossed the scarf and envelope inside. Grace slammed down the lid, feeling a bit of relief having it out of sight.

She splashed cold water over her face and neck and changed shirts before heading down to the clinic. Tyler had asked her not to schedule any morning appointments.

He'd given Shane a clean bill of health, purchased a new collar, and attached an identification tag and the rabies tag, which jangled whenever the dog moved.

When Grace reached the clinic, Tyler was waiting for her beside the truck. His face lit with a boyish grin. "Ready to surprise Mr. Jacobson?"

She nodded, eager to be on the way. She pasted a smile on her face, hoping she showed no signs of the stress twisting her stomach. Tiffany ran to the truck when Tyler lifted Shane inside the cab.

"No, girl, you can't go," Grace said.

Tiffany sat down, a forlorn look on her face. "We'll be back soon. You go visit Brad."

Tiffany's ears perked at the sound of Brad's name.

Grace pointed at the path. "Go."

Tiffany whuffed and bounded off.

Sitting next to Tyler, Grace felt the darkness begin to lift. Of course it was the anticipation of surprising Mr. Jacobson, not because Tyler kept glancing her way. She pretended not to notice, but each time his arm brushed hers, she received a jolt of awareness. Shane sat quietly between them, but Grace kept her arm securely around the dog's midsection, steadying him on the seat. The drive was endlessly long and entirely too short. Her cheeks ached from the smile frozen on her face when Tyler finally pulled into Mr. Jacobson's driveway.

Will came outside the moment Tyler stopped the truck.

"Hi, Doc." He shaded his eyes with one hand. "Something wrong?"

Tyler opened Grace's door. She jumped down and Shane followed. She held tight to the leash as the dog strained to reach Mr. Jacobson.

"We brought you a visitor," Tyler said.

The old man stepped carefully down the last step. "Visitors are always welcome. Come on in."

Shane sniffed Mr. Jacobson's trousers, then licked his hand.

Will chuckled. "Well, now, you're a good lookin' dog. You can come in, too." He glanced at Grace. "Welcome back, young lady. You folks feel up to some home made lemonade?"

Grace kissed his cheek. "It's good to see you, Mr. Jacobson."

"Will," he corrected. "Mr. Jacobson was my pa. Now how about a cool drink?"

Grace smiled. "I'd love a glass of lemonade, Will."

"Me, too," Tyler said.

Will led them into the house and pulled out chairs encouraging them to sit. "What's your dog's name?" he asked.

Tyler grinned. "That's up to you."

"Eh? How's that?"

"He's all yours," Grace said holding out the leash.

Will looked from Grace to Tyler and back again. Tears shimmered behind his glasses.

"Mine?"

Grace nodded, feeling tears smart behind her eyes, too.

Will reached down and petted the dog's head. "Well, now." Will's voice cracked. "I'm pleased to have you, if you want to stay," he said to the dog.

Shane licked his hand.

"But I'm fresh out of names, I'm afraid."

"We've been calling him Shane," Grace offered.

"Shane," Will repeated.

The dog lifted his ears.

"Shane, it is then. That's a fine name for a fine dog."

Shane barked approval.

****

Grace managed to get through the rest of the day without Tyler suspecting anything. He asked her to stay for dinner, but she declined, saying she had chores and errands to run. He seemed disappointed, but said he understood. When he leaned forward as if to kiss her, she turned her head, pretending not to notice.

As Grace topped the hill, she called Tiffany's name. When there was no answer, her concern grew. She hadn't seen her dog since this morning when she told her to go find Brad. Grace placed her hands on each side of her mouth and called again. "Tiffany!"

Grace ran to the back of the house, hoping to find the dog sleeping in her favorite spot. The sight that met her eyes stopped her flight. Tiffany lay in a pool of blood, the discarded silk scarf knotted around her neck.

Fear and rage battled, fear that her beloved pet might die, rage at the monster who did this, and above it all, a sorrow deep in her heart. Grace dropped to her knees and placed her ear against Tiffany's stomach. A slow but steady heartbeat gave her hope.

"Thank God."

The open hip wound was deep and long, the fur matted with blood.

"It's okay, girl. I'll get help. Tyler will know what to do."

Tiffany's tail wagged once.

Retracing her earlier route, she flew past the outreaching branches, ignoring the sting as they flogged her face. "No, no, no," she chanted with each heavy footfall. She met resistance when she pushed against the clinic door. Damn, it was locked.

She turned, ran down the steps and around the building. Taking the stairs two at a time, she reached the deck and called out, "Tyler! Help!"

****

"Dad, I'll call you later. I've got an emergency." Tyler hung up the phone and walked toward the kitchen. He collided with Grace and grabbed her arms to keep from tumbling to the floor. He touched a red welt on her cheek. "What's wrong, honey?"

"Come quick...Tiffany's hurt. I think she's been stabbed."

What the—?

Grace tugged his arm. "Hurry, she's bleeding. You

109

have to do something. Please, Tyler, you have to come with me."

By the time he retrieved his medical bag, Grace was gone. He caught sight of her running toward the wooded path, and though he was in great shape, he had a difficult time catching up. Tyler followed, and breathless, knelt beside the dog. She had a large wound on her hip, and she'd lost a significant amount of blood. He listened and heard a steady heartbeat. A good sign, but he couldn't risk moving her until he stopped the bleeding. He clipped around the wound and cleaned it as best he could. He fingered the scarf knotted around the dog's neck wondering where it had come from.

Grace yelled into the trees as if someone stood there. "I swear I'm going to kill you." Her hands clamped into fists. "You stinking coward. I'll cut out your heart for doing this. You hear me! You're a dead man!"

Chills ran down Tyler's spine. Grace tipped back her head and emitted a scream that left him raw and wounded. He put his arms around her, drawing her to his chest. Her body stiffened against him. "It's all right, honey. She's going to be okay, but we have to get her to the clinic right away." He stroked the wild silky curls on Grace's head, whispering over and over that Tiffany would be fine. Slowly she began to relax, her body leaning into him. He tipped her face to his and kissed her. His arms trembled with the force of his emotions. He couldn't bear Grace's pain. He looked into her eyes, now gleaming with unshed tears. "I promise she won't die. I won't let that happen. You hear me?"

Her arms wrapped around his waist and she dropped her forehead to his chest.

"Grace. Do you trust me?"

She nodded.

His heart felt like a heavy rock in his chest. She trusted him, and he had to follow through on his promise. But once she learned the truth about him, she'd never trust him again. He couldn't think of that now though.

Now he had to help Tiffany.

"Can you get me a blanket?" he asked.

She sniffed. Her eyes met his and he saw flecks of midnight blue far behind the surface, pulling him in, drowning him in their depths. She nodded.

Moments later, she returned with a lightweight blanket.

Together they eased Tiffany onto the blanket. He wrapped it around the dog and carefully lifted her in his arms. "Will you carry my bag?"

Grace grabbed it and followed him down the steps.

"Tyler, is she really going to be all right?"

The tremor in her voice tugged at his heartstrings. He was positive the injury wasn't accidental. Someone *had* stabbed the dog, and he was afraid he knew who had performed the evil deed. "She's going to make it, babe."

Two hours later, Tiffany lay sedated but out of danger. Grace sat in a chair outside the cage, her hand resting on her dog's head. Tyler kept an eye on her while he cleaned up.

"Are you sure she's going to make it?"

"Absolutely. Tomorrow she'll be more alert, but we'll have to keep her caged for a few days."

Grace nodded. "Thank you. I'll pay you for this, I promise."

He gritted his teeth. Hadn't they gone beyond being business associates? Hoping the frustration didn't reach his voice, he replied, "I love that dog nearly as much as you. There's no charge, Grace. Come on, let's get something to eat."

"I'm not hungry."

"Then keep me company while I eat. Tiffany is fine. She's going to sleep through the night."

"I'm not leaving her alone." She glanced up at him and the anger he saw made him step back.

He didn't blame her. What happened to the dog wasn't an accident. "We need to notify the authorities about what happened."

"No. I can handle this myself."

"Grace—"

"I said no."

He took a deep breath and ran his hand through his hair. She was in no mood to listen to reason. Did she know who had done this? "Grace, did you put this on Tiffany?" He held up the scarf he'd removed from the dog's neck.

Her face drained of color. "It's mine. I think I left it at Brad's. He must have returned it via Tiffany."

She was lying. He read it in her posture and in her eyes. Why? What significance did the scarf have? He tossed it to her and she balled it up and stuffed it in her pocket.

"So why don't you want to notify the authorities?"

"Why should I? Couldn't the wound be accidental? What if she got into a trap? Or got into a tangle with another animal? I mean, who would deliberately hurt my dog? It doesn't make sense."

"The wound was a clean cut. It looks like a knife wound. That isn't accidental."

She placed her hands on her hips. "And you're an expert on knife wounds?"

He shrugged. "All I'm telling you is that it looks too clean to have been caused by another animal. A trap would have caused more damage, maybe broken her leg—" He held out his hand when she opened her mouth to protest. "And if it was a trap it would have been lower, not up on the hip."

"And I'm telling you to let it go. There isn't a soul in Foxfire who would hurt her, not deliberately. All I care about is getting her back on her feet. Then I'll decide how to protect her in the future."

She walked out of the room and looked back over her shoulder. "Didn't you mention getting something to eat? Suddenly I'm famished."

Tyler gave up. They went to his apartment and he pulled eggs and bacon from the refrigerator. Grace started a pot of coffee. They worked together and when the food was done, they carried it to the deck. Tyler lit the gas torches. He couldn't let Grace go back home tonight. His gut told him Max had something to do with what happened, and he thought Grace knew it, too. He'd been too aware of her reaction over the scarf. It wasn't hers. What part did it play in the whole scenario? Damn. He needed to talk to Jake. Maybe it was time to tell Grace the truth. She deserved to know. If he could just get her to stay with him for the night, then tomorrow morning he'd lay everything out on the table when she'd be ready to listen. If it meant she didn't want to pursue the attraction between them, he'd just have to accept it. The important thing was to protect her.

"Will you stay here tonight? I know you'd like to be close to Tiffany. My couch makes into a bed. I can sleep there and give you my bedroom." He tried to lighten the air. "I promise not to let you seduce me."

She glanced down at her rumpled blood-stained clothing. "If you really don't mind, that will ease my mind. But I can't let you give up your bed. I'll take the sofa." He started to protest, but decided not to push his luck.

"Okay," he agreed.

She stood and carried her plate to the kitchen. "Thanks for dinner. I'll just go shower and get a change of clothes."

"You're not going anywhere alone."

"I don't need—"

"Remember what I told you about my mother?"

"But—"

"Grace. Be reasonable. It will only take a few minutes to drive to your place. Let me do that much for you."

She stared into his eyes. Finally she shrugged. "Whatever. But let's go check on Tiffany first."

****

Grace spent a restless night on Tyler's couch. At the first sign of light, she washed her face, brushed her teeth, and finger-combed her damp curls. There was no sound coming from behind Tyler's closed bedroom door, so she quietly went about putting on a pot of coffee.

Tyler's apartment was surprisingly homey, more so than her house which she'd had three years to decorate and furnish. In the back of her mind lurked the possibility of having to move. At times it seemed she'd spent her entire life running away from something. Though she told herself she'd never run again, that she'd stay in Foxfire forever, reality had her poised for flight. Perhaps it would be best to leave Foxfire as soon as Tiffany recovered. If Max wanted her, he'd have to find her again and she wouldn't have the guilt of endangering her friends. The thought of never seeing Brad again started a throbbing tension headache. Max had already stolen so much from her. She deserved a life free from his threat.

Grace lifted a silver filigree frame from the mantle. The image of a man and woman smiled back at her. This had be a picture of Tyler's parents. The woman's green eyes were the mirror image of Tyler's, and the man's teasing dimples, she'd seen many times on Tyler's face. She sighed. She didn't want to give up her life here.

Tyler's voice drifted through his closed bedroom door. She set the picture back in place and cautiously approached.

"No, don't send anyone yet. I'll call if I need help. If Max is here, I'll get him."

Max? She placed her ear against the door. Who was Tyler talking to, and what did he know about Max?

"I'm not sure Max is behind this yet."

Grace's heart began to thud loudly.

"Although Max prefers guns, I think it was him. Whoever did it was lashing out at Grace. She and that dog are inseparable."

Grace turned the knob on the bedroom door and flung it open. She had a second to register the slam against the wall before Tyler dropped the phone and spun, both hands closed around a gun pointed right between her eyes.

"Damn," he said, lowering the weapon. He picked up the phone with one hand. "I'll call you back." He dropped it back on the mattress and shoved the gun in his waistband.

Grace's shock began to ebb. "Who the hell are you?"

Tyler ruffled a hand through his hair. "I guess you overheard."

"I didn't overhear. I *eavesdropped*. I want answers, Tyler."

His gaze burned into hers. "Let me fix some coffee first."

She blocked the doorway. "Who are you? A cop?"

His closed expression showed no sign of what he might be thinking. "No," he replied. He gently moved her aside and strode toward the kitchen.

Grace tagged closely behind. "Are you really a vet?"

"Thanks." He nodded toward the full pot of coffee and reached for the cabinet door. Grace's hand stopped him from opening it.

"Answers first."

"Yes, I'm a vet."

"What else?"

He pulled out a chair and indicated she should do the same. Deep in her soul, she feared her world was about to come crashing in on her.

"I'll tell you everything you want to know after I have a cup of coffee."

He ran a hand through his hair again, leaving it mussed. Much to her dismay, it reminded her of soft beds and sex. "It's been a rough night."

How could he appear so calm and unconcerned after pointing a gun at her? The hard look in his eyes as he'd spun with the weapon in his hands told her he knew how to use it. She had to get away from him and from the past that knocked harshly on the locked door of her heart. "Yes, it has," she responded. The urge to run overpowered her desire to hear his explanations. "To hell with the coffee. And to hell with you!" She whirled and ran for the sliding doors.

****

Tyler reacted on instinct, grabbing her arm. She drove a fist into his nose, surprising him and loosening his fingers. She pulled free and darted outside.

He tested his nose for blood, found none, and hurried after her. A brief smile tugged at his lips. The woman might be small, but she packed a mean right hook.

He caught her at the edge of the woods, and grabbed her from behind, wrapping his arms around her waist and lifting her from the ground.

She fought hard, slamming her head back, trying to connect with his face. Her feet kicked against his shins and her breath came in short grunts of frustration.

"Let. Me. Go." She clawed at him.

Her nails raked his arm. "Damn it, Grace. Give me a chance to explain."

"No." Her head slammed against his chest. She nailed a solid kick to his shin, staggering him.

He dropped to the ground, pinning her beneath him. Her weight was no match against him, and she wilted, closing her eyes and turning her face away.

"I'm not a cop. I'm a vet. And I work for...a private investigation firm."

She opened her eyes and spit in his face.

So much for thinking she'd given in to his superior position. He wiped a hand across his face. Her eyes glared through him like poison darts.

"You're investigating me?" she yelled.

He'd expected her anger, but not the hatred sparking deep in her eyes. Somehow that hurt more than her punch to his nose.

"Just let me explain." He drew in a deep breath. "If I let you go, will you promise not to run away?"

"Why should I?"

"Have you forgotten about Tiffany?"

Her gaze wavered. She shifted, trying to free herself.

His body responded. Looking down into her flushed face and angry eyes brought a desire to mash his lips on hers and turn her anger into a passion that would drive them both over the edge. He shook his head, wishing he dared to let go of her long enough to regain his senses. He groaned inwardly as the pressure against his zippered jeans increased. "I am a vet, Grace." She pushed against him and he grunted.

"Let me up." She bucked upward.

"Can I trust you?" he asked.

"Can I trust *you*?" she countered.

"Yes." Slowly, he raised his body off hers, stood and extended his hand to help her up.

She ignored his gesture and pushed to her feet.

He wiped the perspiration from his brow. "Can we have that coffee now?"

Grace dusted her backside then turned and strode back to his apartment.

****

When they reached the deck, Grace leaned against the railing, while Tyler went inside. Anger raged, making her want to hit something, or someone—namely Tyler. He'd lied to her. Had anything he'd told her been truthful? Fury built in her chest until she wanted to release her frustration in a blood-curdling scream. She wouldn't give in to the temptation. Only a woman who had no recourse would resort to such an outlet. Grace had years of experience in stifling her true feelings. She pushed back the surface emotions, determined to find out the truth.

Tyler returned and handed her a cup of coffee. The last thing she needed was caffeine. For a moment, she contemplated flinging the hot liquid in his face, then turned her back before the temptation overcame her.

"I didn't mean to infer you were my case," Tyler said, his voice too near for comfort.

She inched away, putting more distance between them. "So, I'm not your case?"

"No."

She turned and glared at him through narrowed eyes.

He threw up his arms. "All right. You're my case." He flopped into a chair. "Sit down, Grace."

She pressed her lips together. She took orders from no man.

He heaved a loud and obviously frustrated breath of air. "I moved to Foxfire to start a veterinarian practice. I needed to make a new start. I was sick of working undercover, and there were too many bad memories in Ohio."

"What does that have to do with me?" She fought to keep the anger under control.

"Max Clayton."

She felt a nerve twitch beneath her eye. "I don't know anyone named Max," she lied.

"Three people have been murdered. All of them testified in the trial." A muscle jumped in his clenched jaw. "We think Max fled the country after his escape, but he's back now, maybe with a new face."

Murdered? She felt the blood draining from her face, and in spite of the heat, a chill crept into her bones.

Tyler's penetrating gaze never left hers. "You're the last person alive who testified in the trial."

"And you think I'm next?"

Tyler stood and touched her shoulder.

She pulled away. "Don't touch me."

"I want to help you."

"Help me? How? By lying to me? Seducing me?" She paced to the opposite of the deck. How could he use her like that? She wanted to blame him for everything, but hadn't she kept secrets, too? This was her fault. She'd let herself be used again.

In a low controlled voice she said, "If you'd told me the truth, Tiffany wouldn't be lying in a cage fighting for her life." She approached and pushed her hands against his chest.

He took a staggering step backwards. "Damn it,

Grace. We need to talk, not throw accusations around."

"Talk? About your lies? About how you deceived me and everyone else who befriended you?"

She took a deep breath. She knew she wasn't being fair. An overwhelming sense of doom surrounded her. She sank into one of the chairs and dropped her face into her hands. She would not cry. She was as much to blame as Tyler. She hadn't told him the truth either. And she knew Max had sent her the scarf. "You think he's here? In Foxfire?"

"Yes."

"What makes you so sure you can catch him?" she asked quietly.

"It's my job."

She blew out a breath. Her stomach felt like she'd just gotten over a bad episode of food poisoning. "Damn."

Tyler went inside and brought out the pot of coffee. "Will you tell me what you can about Max?"

She straightened and looked into his eyes. Why not? Maybe it would help him to find the bastard. What did it matter if he looked at her with contempt when she finished?

She took a deep breath and began to tell her story.

"I met him when I was working as a cocktail waitress. He's the type who could charm a snake without using a flute." She shrugged. "So, when he asked me to have dinner with him, I accepted. I didn't have a clue about his illegal activities then."

She tried to read Tyler's face to see if he believed her. It shouldn't matter, but it did. "After that it seemed he showed up every night I worked. We began spending lots of time together. For my birthday, he gave me a diamond and sapphire necklace. Needless to say I was impressed with his wealth. He could give me all the things I'd never had. Security, someone to take care of me for a change."

Tyler didn't say a word. He just sat back in the chair, crossed his ankles and sipped coffee.

"We became...close." She couldn't bring herself to say

she'd slept with him. "It wasn't long before I began to suspect he was into drugs. Call it intuition or stupidity. I knew he and Manny Bonino were friends, and Manny was always one step ahead of the law. They arrested him for drug trafficking several times, but his attorney always got him off."

Tyler kept his gaze fixed securely on hers. He sipped his coffee, making no comment.

"I tried to break it off with him. Told him I didn't want to see him anymore. I even offered to give him back the necklace. He wouldn't let me go. He kept calling and dropping by the club. One night, he was waiting in the shadows outside my apartment when I got home. I didn't see him until I opened the door, and he slammed inside with Manny."

Grace took a drink of lukewarm coffee. "I was scared. I knew I could handle one of them, but not two. Manny had a knife and he held it to my throat. Max just laughed. I tried to fight, but Max put a cloth over my mouth and I passed out. When I woke up, I was a prisoner in his brothel."

She searched Tyler's face for his reaction, but saw nothing that told his feelings. She continued.

"I know it sounds like a trumped up story, but it's the truth. When I woke up, I was locked in a bedroom. I tried to open the window, but it wouldn't budge. I think it might have been glued shut or something. I even tried to break it, but the only thing that broke was the lamp. No one even came to investigate. Later that night a young girl opened the door. I told her I'd been brought there under force."

Grace held out her cup for fresh coffee. Tyler poured it without saying a word.

"She didn't seem surprised. She said Max wanted to talk to me." Grace met Tyler's penetrating gaze. "That girl couldn't have been a day over sixteen. She led me to a room at the end of a long hall and left me alone with Max. When I looked into his eyes, I wondered how I ever saw anything charming about him. I hated him. He was arrogant and so damn sure he had me trapped. But I turned the tables on him, used his ego to my advantage."

Did Tyler understand what she meant? Their gazes locked. Why didn't he say something? Anything? She swallowed hard. The truth was, she'd let Max use her that night. She'd been a willing partner, though she'd kept her mind above the act.

"When he was...preoccupied, I stabbed him with a letter opener I'd taken off the desk. Then I hit him with the brass lamp and called 911. The rest is history. The cops gave me immunity for testifying against him."

She stared into his eyes. "Now you know the whole story. You know who I am, what I am. What more do you want to know?"

He reached for her hand. "Thanks for telling me." She didn't see disgust clouding his eyes. He smiled at her, his thumb caressing the back of her hand. "It doesn't change how I feel about you, but it does make a few things clearer."

"What things?"

"Why Max is so determined to find you."

She drew her hand away. "Do you think he stabbed Tiffany?"

"That's what Jake believes."

"Jake?"

"Jake Scott. He's head of a department in the Drug Enforcement Agency."

"That's who you work for, the DEA?"

He nodded. "Temporarily." He refilled his cup. "Natalie introduced us. She was Jake's sister...and my wife."

"Wife?" He was married? Hurt gnawed deep in her chest.

"I worked for Jake to pay my way through school. Dad was a small town vet, and when Mom developed cancer it took all their savings to pay the medical bills. After I graduated, I went to work with dad, but I still worked undercover assignments for Jake, too. Then Natalie and I got married."

"And you quit working for your...wife's brother?"

"No."

Grace ran a finger around the rim of her mug. "You worked for your dad and the agency at the same time?"

"Yes. I was part of the team assigned to dig into Max's businesses." Tyler leaned forward, capturing her gaze. "After Max's arrest, I wanted to make sure he was convicted. I attended the trial."

"Were you there when I testified?"

"Yes."

She raised her eyebrows. "You're telling me you worked with the authorities and you let Max get away?" Was that guilt she read crossing his face?

He intertwined his fingers and dropped his hands between his knees before replying. "Natalie called my cell phone right after we received the announcement that the jury had reached a verdict. She asked me to come home because she had something important to tell me that she couldn't share over the phone." He swallowed and his Adam's Apple bounced. "I told her I couldn't come home until after the trial closed." He tipped his head back and took a deep breath.

Grace watched emotions chase across his features. "What does that have to do with Max's escape?"

He ran his fingers through his hair. "Natalie decided not to wait. She arrived at the courtroom when the jury foreman read the verdict. The whole place erupted in chaos. That's when Max made his escape. Before they could handcuff him, he grabbed a woman and used her as a shield."

Grace knew what he was going to say. She wanted to stop him, ease the pain radiating from his eyes.

"It was only after they found her body that I learned the woman was Natalie."

"My God." She reached out to him, placing a hand on his arm.

"She was pregnant. That's the news she wanted to share."

"I'm sorry, Tyler." She wasn't sure what she felt. Sympathy certainly. Yet something nibbled at her heart. He'd been in love with another woman. Had planned on having a family. He'd lost his dream, too, but not of his own doing. His dream had been snatched away by a horrid senseless murder. Grace had murdered her own dream by the choices she'd made. Still, her heart ached for his loss.

He pulled his arm from under her grip. "Max headed the biggest drug and prostitution ring in Columbus. We had him and he got away. He disappeared and we weren't able to track him until three months ago. A body was found in an alley on the near East side. A woman. She'd been shot in the forehead. The police added it to a long line of prostitution and drug-related murders...until another body was pulled out of the Scioto river—another woman. Same caliber gun. Both of them had testified against Max."

Grace said, "He told me he'd get even for my betrayal. I didn't know he'd come after anyone but me. I ran away. I stayed in Missouri for a while until I had enough money to make a new start. Then I came here."

"We searched for you and Ted Powell since you were the last two people alive who'd testified at Max's trial. So, when your picture appeared in the paper—"

Grace leaned forward. "My picture? What do you mean?"

"You and Connor Thomas."

"But that was local news."

"Ever hear of the internet?"

"That's how you found me?" How could that be? She'd never even given a thought to having her picture in the paper. Her heart dove toward her stomach. "Then that's how Max found me, too."

"And that's why I came to Foxfire. I'd been talking about leaving the agency and going back into veterinarian

123

practice. After Natalie...I felt so guilty for letting her down that I focused all my time on catching Max. But I was getting burned out. There'd been no sign of Max, and I was sick of spending all my time dealing with the dregs of the world. And I was sick of Ohio and all the memories I couldn't shake."

Tyler tipped his head back against the chair. "Night and day all I could think about was Max. He stole my life. I wanted it back. So I told Jake I was going to move away and start over. He begged me to take one last assignment, and he made it irresistible with the idea of opening my own clinic, so I decided this would be as good a place as any to start over."

"Did you hire me because of Max?" She lifted her chin and met his gaze full-on.

Tyler jumped to his feet. He raked a hand through his hair. "No."

"But you're using me as bait, right?"

"God, no, Grace. How can you think that?"

"How can I not? But, I don't blame you," she said.

He knelt in front of her. "I swear the last thing I want to do is hurt you."

She stared into his eyes. "It's too late."

"I'm not going to use you to get Max."

"It doesn't matter if you do or not."

"It matters to me." His gaze held her in place.

She slowly shook her head. "How can you expect me to believe you?"

He touched her cheek with the barest brush of his fingers. "Grace, I came here expecting to find a woman with a heart of steel and a ruthless mind. But that's not what I found. I found a woman with a heart of gold and a compassionate soul."

Soft shivers raced through her body and pooled in her abdomen.

He said, "This isn't about catching Max anymore."

"What is it about?"

"I wish I knew."

"Stop looking for things that don't exist. I'm tarnished, Tyler. I'm to blame, not Max. I made the decision to believe in him, he didn't force me to care. I closed my eyes to the truth around me because I wanted what he had to offer. Don't you see what kind of woman that makes me?"

"Stop putting yourself down. I don't care what happened in your past. I care about you. The real you."

Even as her heart swelled with hope, she denounced herself for being a fool.

"You don't know the real me."

"I know you make me feel things I have no right to feel."

She pushed past him. "That's only lust," she said. "It'll go away. *Trust* me."

"That's the biggest problem of all. I do trust you, Grace. And that scares the hell out of me."

An ache settled in Grace's heart. He'd lost his wife and child. He'd been hurt by Max even more than she had.

"When were you planning on telling me?"

"This morning."

She smirked.

"It's the truth. I swear. Last night I wanted to tell you, especially after seeing your reaction to the scarf—"

She turned away and he pulled her back to face him. "Tell me about the scarf, Grace."

She shook her head. "It's nothing."

"It's something. Tell me."

Grace took a deep breath. "Yesterday I found an envelope in my mailbox. The scarf was inside with a message from Max."

His eyes widened. "What message?"

She shrugged. "Just a note to let me know he'd found me."

"Where is it?"

"I threw everything away. Max must have pulled the scarf out of the trash and put it around Tiffany's neck as a warning to me."

"What did the note say?"

"Not much. I was so shocked I can't remember exactly what he wrote."

"I need to see it."

"All right." She took a deep breath. "Look, I'll help you find Max. Whatever it takes. I just want my life back."

Tyler touched her cheek. "I won't let you put yourself in danger."

"I'm already in danger. And it won't stop until Max is caught." She smiled. "I'm not worth worrying about. Let's go check on Tiffany, then we can get the note. And I want to talk to Brad, too."

Tyler nodded. "All right."

"Tyler, Max is the one who left the roses, not Adam."

He squeezed her shoulders. "We'll get him."

They went to the clinic and Grace touched Tiffany's silky fur. "Is she still under the sedative?"

"I gave her another shot last night while you were sleeping, but she'll wake up soon."

Grace wanted nothing more than to lean against his chest and forget her doubts, her fears, her pain, but she couldn't allow herself to trust him—not yet.

"When?" she asked.

"In an hour or so, but we'll have to keep her confined for a few days."

He placed a finger beneath her chin, forcing her to look into his eyes. "Grace, she's going to be fine."

She nodded. She couldn't speak over the lump in her throat. She really needed Brad now. He'd always been the first person she turned to whenever anything good or bad occurred in her life. She pulled away.

"Let's go. I really need to see Brad." She spun to face him. "Does he know?" she asked.

His forehead scrunched into a puzzled frown. "About Tiffany?"

"No, about you being a..." She waved her hands.

"Whatever you are."

He touched her face, the look in his eyes softening. "You say that like I've grown scales or pointed teeth."

She swatted his hand. "You deceived me. You deceived all of us." She pulled away, wiping a hand across her forehead and pushing her hair away from her face. "I even let you kiss me and...God, how could I have been so stupid?"

She wasn't being fair, but she couldn't allow Tyler to have any illusions about them. Not while a threat of Max existed. She couldn't bear the thought of Max hurting Tyler. The last piece of her shattered heart mended as she realized she had fallen in love with him.

"I wasn't pretending." He stared at her, his eyes so intense they smoldered like emerald fire. "I wanted to make love to you, Grace."

He took her hand and led her out the door.

Chapter Ten

Max rubbed the area on his face that, thanks to a skilled plastic surgeon, no longer sported a long jagged scar. The surgeon had also restructured his nose, removing the hook he'd always hated. Why not? He'd never had a problem getting women, but the scar on his face would have marked him forever—a constant reminder of what that bitch had done.

He'd taken care of the others, the imbeciles who thought they'd beaten him by testifying against him. He'd shown them, hadn't he? He'd escaped right under their noses. Max didn't lose, nor did he forget. They thought they'd beaten him by freezing the assets in his accounts. The idiots didn't realize they were up against a genius. He'd spent the past three years on his fortress island that no one could penetrate. He'd tossed around the idea of taking Grace there, using her until he broke her spirit, but he came up with a better plan. He'd found he liked killing with a knife even better than using a gun.

Everything was falling into place. These back-country bumpkins were tripping over their own feet trying to catch the Knoxville Knifer. He wanted to laugh aloud at their ignorance. No one could recognize Max with his new face, not even Grace. She'd come nose to nose with him outside the D.A.'s office and hadn't blinked an eye.

Footsteps sounded on the path. He fell back, deeper into cover of the trees. The old man hurried past Max's hiding place and disappeared around a bend. He supposed Grace's friends were gathering round to pay respects to the dead dog. Pity that. He really liked dogs, but he needed to get Grace's attention.

He had that now. Yes indeed. He felt a grin lift the corners of his mouth. Time was on his side, and it was quickly running out for Grace.

****

"There's Brad now." Grace ran to him.

"Grace! Are you all right?" His lined face gave voice to his worry. He opened his arms and she stepped into his comforting embrace.

"Not really," she said, her words muffled against his chest.

"What's wrong, honey?" he murmured.

"Tiffany's hurt." She felt his muscles tighten. "Somebody stabbed her."

"What?"

Brad stepped back and looked at Tyler. "Is she...?" His words trailed off.

"She'll be good as new in a few days," Tyler answered.

"So he says," Grace mumbled.

"I'm sorry, darlin'," Brad said. He laid an arm around her shoulder and squeezed. "I've been worried about you. I called several times last night and got your answering machine. I was just heading down to the clinic to see if you were there."

"I stayed with Tyler last night."

Brad's gaze bounced between Tyler and Grace. "What happened? You say Tiffany was stabbed?"

"I found her on the back deck yesterday."

Tyler spoke up. "We need to talk, Brad. Grace, do you mind calling and canceling our appointments for the day?"

"We don't have any, remember? This is your day for volunteer work at the shelter."

"I forgot. I'll call and see if they can do without me today."

"Can we talk at my house?" Brad asked. "Something tells me this is going to take a while and I'm waiting on a call from Harri."

"You two go on. I'll join you as soon as I make a few

calls." Tyler looked at Grace. "Don't forget to get that envelope and note."

"I won't."

Tyler jogged back toward the clinic and Brad put an arm around her waist. "What's all this about an envelope and note?"

"Come on, I'll show you." Grace lifted the lid on the garbage can, but all that remained inside was a plastic bag of trash still neatly secured. The envelope and note were gone. Reaching inside she moved the bag to see if the papers had slipped to the bottom. No, they were definitely missing and along with them any proof that Max had contacted her. She calmly replaced the lid, hiding her fear from Brad. She took his arm. "Let's go to your house. There's so much to tell you, but I need a bowl of ice cream."

Tyler joined them a few minutes later but declined the dessert. "Where's the note?"

"It's gone. Max must have taken it when he took the scarf."

Brad turned a puzzled frown on them. "What's going on here? Max? Is that man here? For God's sake, honey, we've got to call the sheriff."

Grace looked at Tyler. "Tell him who you are."

****

Tyler closed his eyes and prayed for patience. He'd gambled on telling Grace the truth, but in doing so, he'd hurt her and maybe ruined any chance of keeping her in his life. But Grace's safety came above his personal feelings. Above all else, he swore he'd keep Grace out of Max's reach.

"I'm an undercover agent for the DEA in Ohio. But it's only temporary. As soon as I catch Max, I'm retiring to spend the rest of my life working here as a veterinarian. Jake, that's my boss, and I have been after Max since he escaped from the courtroom where he'd been convicted of several crimes." Tyler paused and searched for the words he needed to say. "I was married to Jake's sister."

Brad's eyes shifted quickly to Grace. Tyler watched the silent exchange between them.

"Max took a woman hostage for protection until he could escape. After he had her drive him away from the city, he killed her and left her body alongside the road. That was his first murder. Since then, he's killed all the people who testified against him, with the exception of Grace. That's why I came to Foxfire."

As if he heard nothing after the word married, Brad said, "Are you divorced?"

Tyler was surprised to feel Grace's hand grip his. "No. The woman Max took captive was Tyler's wife. Max killed her. And she was pregnant."

Brad's face lost color. "Tyler, I'm sorry."

Tyler shook his head. "It's been three years. I've come to terms with it. The important thing is that Grace is in danger. We need to protect her."

"Son, I'm really sorry," Brad said. "Dealing with her death must have been hard. I know."

"Like I said, it happened a long time ago. My only concern now is Grace."

"I agree. We can't leave her alone. Somebody's got to be with her at all times."

"Right," Tyler agreed.

"Wait a minute. Don't I have a say in this?" Grace asked.

"No," both men answered in unison.

"Listen. I'm not some helpless female. I know Max and I know how dangerous he is, but I'm not defenseless. I've taken self-defense courses. I have a gun and—"

"Whoa," Tyler interrupted. "*You* have a gun?"

"Of course. I've been running and hiding from Max for a long time. I had to protect myself."

"Do you have a license?"

"Yes, and I know how to shoot."

Great. Tyler didn't have to think twice about how dangerous that might be. Not to Max, but to Grace. Didn't she realize Max could overpower her and use the gun against her? "Grace, I don't doubt you know how to protect yourself, but I'm not willing to take any chances. From now until we catch Max, you're going to stay with me."

"And how is that going to help catch Max? He wants *me*, and he's threatened to kill anyone who helps me. That means you, Tyler." She faced Brad. "And you. I'm not willing to risk your life. If it wasn't for me, you'd be safe."

"And I wouldn't have you to love," Brad said. "Grace, you've got to listen to Tyler. He's trained in these things."

Tyler had to hand it to Brad. He'd taken in a lot this afternoon and kept everything in perspective. "Nothing is going to happen to either of you. I'll call Jake and have him send in some men to help."

"Sounds like a plan," Brad agreed.

****

She's in good hands, Brad thought, watching Grace and Tyler walk away together. Grace might pretend she didn't want Tyler's help, but Brad knew she would do anything for Tiffany.

Tyler was a good man, dependable and down-to-earth, nothing like the lawyer Grace had been engaged to. All the things she'd ever wanted were within reach, if she'd only open her eyes and her heart.

Yes, they would make a perfect match. Things would work out once they got past the issues at hand. He went inside to call Adam and invite him down. Adam needed to know what was happening, too. Especially since there would be some strangers coming in later today.

Adam knocked at the door less than five minutes later. Brad joined him on the porch and Adam began to talk before Brad could find a way to tell him what he'd learned.

"Strange things are happening," Adam said.

"Indeed, they are, my friend. Indeed they are."

"It's that vet. Nothing bad ever happened in Foxfire until he came."

"Adam, tell me the truth. Are you in love with

Grace?"

Adam scuffed his foot across the rough boards, like a little boy caught in a lie. "I don't love her. Not in the way you mean." He looked at Brad. "I think she's real pretty, and I hoped...but she's not interested in an old man like me. I had a crush, that's all. I realized that when Lainey and I started seeing each other again."

"I see."

"Lainey and I would be married if I hadn't done something stupid."

Neither Adam nor Lainey ever explained why they called off their engagement. Neither of them had dated anyone else since, at least to Brad's knowledge. He'd often wondered what happened, though he'd never brought up the subject with Adam.

Adam took off his cap and held it in his hands. His arms rested on his legs as he leaned forward, his gaze focused on the boards under his feet.

"So, what happened to you and Lainey?" Brad asked.

"Before I tell, you've got to promise not to say a word to her." He turned his gaze on Brad's.

"Okay." Brad nodded as he agreed. He began a slow rocking motion, keeping both feet firmly on the floor.

"She don't want anyone to know."

"Then maybe you shouldn't tell me," Brad said.

Adam's eyebrows shot upward. "I trust you, Brad, and I need somebody to talk to."

Brad patted Adam on the back. "I trust you too, my friend."

"Cross your heart," Adam ordered.

Brad complied with the childish request.

Adam shifted his gaze away. "Lainey and I were sweethearts in school. I always knew we'd get married. Lainey felt the same way. We used to talk about how it would be."

Adam looked out toward the mountains in the distance. "Then Lainey's mom got sick and she had to take care of her while her dad went to work." Adam leaned back in the chair and began to rock. "Grandpa was in the hospital then, too. We both had our hands full."

"I remember that time," Brad said. It had also been when Jenny had been diagnosed with cancer. Sadness crept into his heart for his loss. Jenny had been gone for a long time, but she still lived in his heart and in his memory. Not a day went by that he didn't think of her.

Adam's voice droned on.

"After Lainey's mom got better, I gave Lainey an engagement ring, and we set a date to get married."

Brad remembered the engagement party Lainey's parents hosted. Everyone in Foxfire had attended. Even Jenny, though she'd been so ill. "That was quite a party Lainey's folks threw."

Adam's jaw clenched and unclenched several times "Yeah." Adam popped the knuckles on his left hand.

Brad rocked back and forth.

Adam worried his lip.

Finally, Brad broke the silence. "Let's see. You were going to get married in October, right?"

Adam's eyes widened as they met Brad's. "Not that year. We planned on a long engagement." Adam popped the knuckles on his right hand.

"That's right," Brad said. "You decided to wait a few years...three wasn't it?"

Adam nodded. "And that's what caused the problems between us."

"Whatever it was couldn't have been that bad," Brad ventured.

Adam stared at the floor again. "Yeah, it was."

The wind blew the trees, swaying the tops in a gentle dance beneath a clear blue sky. In the distance, cicadas sang their songs, the notes rising and falling, then picking up again from another direction. Birds chittered, adding to nature's stereo. As Brad rocked, he lost himself in the peaceful sights and sounds of the mountain's majesty, but under it all, he felt the danger closing in on them.

"You'll understand what I did. You're a man." Adam

fixed his gaze on Brad's.

"I'm sure I will," Brad answered, not at all sure if he would.

"Lainey was beautiful. I mean, she still is, but...when she was young, she made my body shake every time we kissed. You know what I mean?"

Brad nodded.

"I'd hold her and kiss her and next thing, my arms would start to shake, then my whole body felt like an earthquake rumbled under my feet. I couldn't stop it for nothing." He looked at Brad with a hint of a smile lighting his eyes. "She knew what she did to me, too." Adam pushed out of the chair and walked to the end of the porch and back, stopping to lean against a pillar. The grooves beside his mouth appeared deeper, and his cheekbones stood out sharply.

"That's a natural feeling, Adam. I felt the same way with Jenny." Brad felt a trembling deep inside whenever he thought about how good things had been between them. That's what kept him from proposing to Harri. He was afraid Jenny's memory would haunt him forever.

Adam slapped his ball cap against his leg. "So, maybe you can understand what I did."

"What did you do, Adam?"

Adam's face turned red. "I peeked in her window and watched her while she was getting dressed. One night she caught me. We argued about it and I told her a man has needs when he loves a woman. I-I touched her breast and pulled her against me so she could feel what she did to me. I tried to stop, Brad, I swear I did." Adam raised his right hand. "But, I couldn't. I kept kissing her. Before I knew it, I'd slipped my hand under her gown. Her skin felt so soft, like velvet."

Adam sank into the rocker. "It didn't matter that she was pushing me away. I was only thinking of me, what I wanted. Until I saw her tears. Then I let her go. I was ashamed of what I'd almost done. I hated the look I'd put in her eyes. She was afraid of me. I knew I'd ruined everything. She threw the ring at me, and that was the end of our engagement."

Brad patted Adam's back. "The important thing is that you stopped, Adam. You didn't want to hurt Lainey."

"You don't know the worst part yet."

Brad didn't think he wanted to hear any more, but Adam needed to get this off his chest. "What is the worst part?"

Adam leaned forward as if sharing a deep secret. "I still watch her."

Adam sat back, his eyes glazing over as if looking at something other then Brad. "At night, I go down to her house and look in her windows. I think she knows I'm there."

Adam blinked. His gaze once more shone brightly on Brad's. "She's not a bad woman, Brad."

"Of course, not," Brad said. He had trouble visualizing Adam as a peeping Tom. "Adam, you know what you're doing is wrong, don't you. You could go to jail."

Adam nodded. "But I can't help myself. Lainey kind of dances before she puts on her nightgown, like she's doing it just for me."

"You aren't peeping through anybody else's windows, are you?"

"No. Why would I do that?"

"You tell me. I'm having trouble believing what I'm hearing."

"Now you're accusing me of doing something I'm not. I thought you'd understand."

"Don't get all riled up again. I wasn't accusing you. I was only asking a question."

"I guess you have the right to ask," Adam conceded. "Anyway, I finally got up the nerve to ask Lainey to dinner and she said yes. She told me she'd forgiven me for what happened. She said she didn't blame me anymore. So we've been spending a lot of time together." Adam leaned forward again. "Last night I stayed at her place."

His eyes shone with a secret happiness. "She was still a virgin. Can you imagine that? She waited for me all these years."

"That's nice, Adam. I'm happy for both of you."

"Yeah, but I still don't know what she sees in a guy like me."

"You and Lainey belong together. Marry the woman while you're still young enough to make memories. Life's too short for second guesses, Adam."

Adam's smile lit his face. "Do you think I should get a new engagement ring or use the old one? I still have it."

Brad patted Adam's hand. "I'd get a new one, my friend. After all, this is a new beginning, right?"

"Right."

Adam and Lainey. Imagine that. After all these years. Brad felt loneliness settle deep in his bones. He'd been alone too long. Maybe he should take his own advice and ask Harri to marry him.

"I'm glad you told me," Brad said. "I hope everything works out for you and Lainey." He began to rock again. "There's something I need to tell you, too. Tyler's an undercover agent who's here to protect Grace."

"He's what?" Adam stared at him as if he'd grown two heads.

"It's true." Brad pushed the rocker back and forth. "He's a vet, too, of course, and he's planning on staying here after he catches the killer."

"Killer?" Adam's voice rose to a near squeal. "The Knoxville Knifer?"

"No, the man Grace has been hiding from. The man who wants to kill her."

And Brad told Adam the entire story.

Chapter Eleven

Outside, a car door slammed. *What now?* Tension riddled Grace to the point of screaming. She sighed and looked at Tyler.

"Somebody's here." Grace had spent the last twenty minutes trying to convince Tyler she could take care of herself. The mental and physical exhaustion had worn her down. She needed a quick shower and time alone. The thought of dealing with one more person was almost more than she could bear.

Resigned to get rid of whoever it was, she headed toward the living room, and Tyler followed.

Harri's sharp glance raked over them. She waited on Grace's doorstep with her hands on her hips and her brightly painted lips pressed together in a straight line. When Grace opened the screen, Harri swept into the house, her orange locks bouncing against an emerald green tank top, which, paired with white shorts, was much tamer than usual. Her shirt matched the shade of Tyler's eyes, vibrantly noticeable when he bent to kiss Harri's cheek.

"How are you, Harri?" he asked.

"Better than you, I suppose," she answered sarcastically. "Now shoo, so Grace and I can talk."

Tyler turned to Grace with a protesting frown.

"Please," Grace said. "I'd like to talk to Harri alone. We can continue our conversation later."

"Trust me, we will," Tyler said, his gaze piercing hers with a make-no-mistake-about-it glare.

Their eyes did a visual battle for an agonizingly long moment before he turned to smile at Harri. "I'll go check on Tiffany."

After the door shut behind him, Harri turned her piercing gaze on Grace.

"Okay, spit it out. What's happened between you and Tyler?" Harri asked.

"Nothing worth mentioning, but Harri, I need your advice."

"That's why I'm here." She lifted her nose and sniffed. "Is that coffee I smell?"

Grace slipped her arm through Harri's. "Come on, I'll get you a cup."

She poured coffee for Harri, then opened the cabinet and pulled out a bag of cookies. She arranged several on the plate before noticing the shocked expression on Harri's face.

"What?" Grace asked, her pulse accelerating.

"You're offering me store-bought cookies?"

Grace looked down at the plate in her hand, then felt a giggle rising.

Harri's brown gaze, filled with mirth, met hers.

"Thanks, Harri. I needed that."

Harri walked forward, took the plate and set it on the table. She wrapped soft, comforting arms around Grace.

Grace absorbed the love emanating from Harri's motherly embrace. If only she could lose herself in the good feelings and forget all the horror of the past twenty-four hours but she couldn't afford to do that. Grace pulled away and gave Harri her best cover-up smile. "You don't have to eat the cookies," she said.

"Oh, fiddle." Harri grabbed the plate and her coffee. Let's go in the living room and get comfortable. We have things to discuss."

Grace sat on the hearth, leaving the rocking chair for Harri.

Harri arranged herself in the chair, crossing her ankles. "I just came from Brad's. Now will you tell me what in the daylights is going on?"

Grace pulled her feet toward her, wrapping her arms around her legs. "Before I say anything else, you've got to promise not to tell Brad."

Harri's hand, gripping the coffee mug, stopped inches from her mouth. She pulled it away without taking a drink. "I tell Brad everything," Harri protested.

"You can't tell him this. Promise me, Harri."

Harri placed the mug on the floor beside her. "We can't leave Brad out of this."

"If you don't promise, then I won't tell you."

As expected, Harri threw up her arms in a dramatic gesture of defeat. "Whatever. I promise." She narrowed her gaze on Grace.

"I have a plan." What she wanted now was to get her life back in order. And she needed Harri's help to do it.

"What plan is that?" Harri asked. She held out her hand, palm toward Grace. "Wait. Don't tell me. You're going to set yourself up as bait."

"Maybe."

"What are you going to do?"

"I have a gun. Max wants me and if I make him believe I'm here alone, he'll come."

"Sure he will, and he'll kill you."

"Not if I have help."

Harri narrowed her eyes. "What kind of help?"

"Yours. You hide in the living room and when he comes, you call Tyler. I'll hold him at gunpoint until Tyler comes and arrests him."

"That's the craziest plan I ever heard. I'm not going to do it and neither are you." Harri pointed a finger at Grace. "I'm not stupid enough to think we can ever pull something like that off. He'll take the gun away from you and shoot us both before help can come. Why don't you ask Tyler to help?"

"Well, it's the best plan I've been able to come up with. Tyler would want to do things his way. You know how men are."

"And he'd be right. I suggest you forget the whole thing. Let Tyler deal with this guy. You stay out of reach."

Maybe it was a stupid idea, but she had to take a

chance. If Harri wouldn't help her, then she'd find a way to do it herself. She decided to change the subject. "Have you heard about Tiffany?"

Harri's face settled into an expression of grief. "Oh, honey, I did. I'm so sorry."

Grace swallowed hard. "She's all right. Tyler took care of her."

"You trust him, then?"

"He's a good vet," she answered.

"That's not what I asked. Do you trust him?"

"I don't know." Grace dropped her forehead to her legs for a second, then lifted her gaze and huffed a breath.

Harri rocked back and forth, creaking the chair against the wooden floor. Her blank gaze seemed to turn inward, then she stopped rocking. Her eyes focused on Grace. "Grace, listen to me. I had a vision. I saw a man with a knife coming after you."

Grace felt the blood rush from her face. "When did you have that vision?"

"Last night. Grace, you're in danger. I've already told Brad about it. That was before I learned about Max being here and Tyler being a secret agent."

"He's not a secret agent."

"Whatever. It doesn't matter. You're in danger. You've got to believe me. This is serious. Nobody believes I'm psychic, but I am."

"I believe you, Harri." And that meant she'd have to face a killer with a knife. Would her self-defense skills help her? No. She shuddered inwardly, remembering the last time she'd been threatened with a knife. She'd have to rely on her gun. And she'd have to be on guard every second.

"Then believe me when I say you have to get out of here. Something bad is about to happen. I can feel it." Harri's strong voice trembled with emotion. "Come stay with me."

"I can't. I need to stay close to Tiffany."

"But you can't stay here alone."

"I can't stay with you or Brad. I won't put you in jeopardy, too."

Grace paced across the room. "Tyler wants me to stay with him. Maybe that's best."

"You have feelings for him, don't you?"

Grace spun around. "Of course I do, but I've always made bad choices when it comes to men. Tyler's no exception."

"I've seen the way he looks at you. He's in love with you."

"Tyler's not in love with me, Harri. He's in love with a ghost."

Harri's eyes lit with interest. "A ghost?"

"His dead wife. Max killed her."

Harri rocked back and forth again. "Max again. Now Tyler's dark aura makes sense. It clouded my reading when I first met him."

"Harri, you exaggerate sometimes, just like Brad says."

"I'm telling you my visions are real. You're in danger, Grace. I think the Knoxville Knifer is planning to make you his next victim. And now you've got that Max guy wanting to get you, too. You need your friends." She leaned forward. "*All* your friends."

A chill slithered up her spine. What connection was there between Max, the Knoxville Knifer, and Harri's vision?

"You're scaring me, Harri."

Harri crossed her arms across her ample chest. "You should be scared. There's something else I know. Tyler's going to save you."

"No man needs to save me, Harri. I can take care of myself."

"Maybe you want to believe you're invincible, but none of us are. Give him a chance."

"I'll try."

"Good. Then let's go to the clinic. I want to see Tiffany."

Grace jumped to her feet. Maybe Tiffany was awake. With all her heart, she hoped so. She needed something positive to focus on.

She locked the door before joining Harri at the bottom of the steps. Grace glanced at Harri's car. "Do you want to drive?"

Harri pulled a pair of sunglasses from her purse and slipped them onto her nose. "Nope. I need the exercise. Let's walk."

A few minutes later, they reached the clinic. Grace slowed when she noticed the absence of Tyler's truck.

"Maybe I should have brought my key. Looks like Tyler's gone," Grace said. "We won't be able to get in."

She walked to the front and tried the door. Sure enough, it was locked. "Maybe we can get in through his apartment. I'll check." She walked down the steps and around the building, stopping abruptly at seeing the infirmary door standing ajar.

Harri pointed. "What about that door?"

Grace's heart leapt to her throat. Tyler wouldn't have left it open.

"Stay here," she ordered.

Grace hurried to the door and barged inside. A man leaned toward the cage where Tiffany lay.

"No!" Grace charged forward but halted in confusion when Adam turned with a smile on his face. The adrenaline rush had her heart pounding and she couldn't believe what she was seeing.

"Look. She likes me, Grace." Adam's hand rested on Tiffany's head. The dog's tail wagged in greeting.

"She's awake."

"Yep. Tyler went into town to get something. I told him I'd keep an eye on her. He says she can't get out and we have to keep her quiet. You're not mad, are you?"

Grace put her hand through the bars and rubbed Tiffany's ears. The dog's tail thumped against the metal cage floor.

"I'm not mad. Looks like you two are friends now."

He grinned. "I'm scared of dogs, especially big dogs." He nodded toward Tiffany. "Like her. But she's not mean. Even if she used to growl at me all the time."

"I think she knew you were afraid of her."

Adam's face flushed. "I guess so, but I'm not afraid of her now. She's a nice dog."

She graced him with a smile.

Harri joined them. "Hi, Adam."

"Hi, Harri." He nodded.

"Looks like Tiffany's better," Harri said.

"Yeah, I should go," Adam said. "You can keep an eye on her until Tyler gets back."

Grace touched Adam's arm. "Thanks for looking after her for me."

Adam looked at her hand resting on his arm. He lifted his gaze to hers and something flickered in their depths. Something Grace didn't want to acknowledge. She snatched her hand to her side.

"You're welcome, Grace." He nodded again at Harri, then left, closing the door firmly behind him.

"That's one strange man," Harri said.

Grace heard tires crunching on the gravel driveway, followed by a door shutting. A few seconds later, Tyler entered the room, a look of surprise on his face.

"Where's Adam?"

"He left," Grace answered.

"And that's what I'm going to do," Harri announced.

"No—" Grace started to protest.

"I promised Brad we'd go to town for an early dinner." She glanced at her watch. "I really should get back to him before he comes looking for me. I have a box of clothes he's going to take to the church for the rummage sale."

Grace didn't want to be alone with Tyler, but it looked like Harri had a different perspective. If she didn't know better, she'd think Harri was matchmaking. Funny that Harri hadn't even liked Tyler in the beginning, but now it seemed as if she'd taken his side...if there were any sides in this ridiculous melodrama.

"I'll walk back with you," Grace volunteered.

"No, dear, that's not necessary." The wicked imp had the audacity to wink.

Grace flicked a glance at Tyler to see if he'd noticed. All she saw was the grim set of his lips. She knew he was going to continue his campaign to keep her in his 'safety zone.'

Harri hugged her and whispered, "Give the man a chance."

Grace had already done that. She wouldn't go there again, no matter what her heart said.

"Don't forget what I told you," Harri said.

"I won't."

When the door closed behind her, Grace turned to follow.

Tyler stopped her, his hand gripping her upper arm. "We have unfinished business."

"You're hurting me." Grace tugged her arm free, and glared into his eyes.

He stepped back. "I didn't mean to hurt you, but you're not going anywhere until we hash out some issues."

"Haven't we already done that?"

Tiffany whined.

Grace hurried back to her cage. "See what you've done?" She turned an angry glare on Tyler. "You're upsetting her. Shouldn't she be kept quiet?"

"She's fine."

Tiffany wagged her tail. Great. Now even her dog was turning against her. Did Tyler have everyone under his spell?

"Come on," Tyler said. "You're not getting away until we finish the discussion we started earlier."

He led the way back to his apartment, where Grace chose to sit in a comfortable chair opposite the sofa. She leaned back, feeling dwarfed and at a disadvantage. Catching the humorous glint in Tyler's eyes, she folded her arms across her chest.

"What more is there to talk about?" she asked.

Tyler sat on the edge of the sofa, placing a bag on the floor at his feet.

Grace flicked a glance at the bag. "What did you buy?"

"An alarm system."

Oh, no. He couldn't possibly have bought that thing for her house.

She rocked forward, placing both feet firmly on the floor. Her hands gripped the arms of the chair. "Don't even tell me that's for my house."

"It is."

"People here do not put in alarm systems. There are no crimes in Foxfire."

His amused glance infuriated her. She wanted to believe Foxfire was safe. That's why she moved here, but she'd brought danger to this community.

"No arguments. If you insist on staying at your place, we've got to do something to make it safe, especially with Tiffany laid up."

Grace knew he was right, but she didn't want to give him the satisfaction. "I don't need an alarm. I have a gun."

His emerald gaze met hers.

She jumped to her feet. "Damn it, Tyler. I don't need you to protect me. I'm perfectly capable of taking care of myself. I've been doing it all my life."

His gaze never wavered. "With a gun?"

She narrowed her gaze. "I know how to handle the gun quite well, thank you."

"And you think you're capable of shooting somebody?"

She held her own. "If I have to."

"Somehow I doubt you'd be able to shoot anyone."

Her face heated. How dare he? Did he really take her for a woman who'd back down from a threat? It just showed how little he really knew her. They could never have a relationship because he was just too cocky, too macho. She didn't need him or any man to protect her.

146

Not now, not ever.

She pulled herself upright. "That's your opinion. I can do anything I set my mind to."

He grinned. "Damned if I don't believe you. So, what did Harri tell you?"

The sudden change of subject took her by surprise.

"Excuse me?"

"Harri said not to forget what she told you."

"Oh, that? You mean I didn't tell you?" she asked in a false disbelieving tone.

"No."

She hitched both shoulders up and down. "Then it must have been none of your business."

Tyler's eyes narrowed into slits and a muscle twitched in his jaw. He stood and moved toward her. She cringed, backing against the chair, preparing to flee. But something about the look in his eyes...something about his demeanor froze her in place. He looked determined and angry...intent on punishing her. Before she could make her move, he grabbed her arms, pulling her toward him and clamping his mouth over hers. The kiss was hot and angry...and breathtaking. He circled her lips with his probing tongue and slipped it into her willing mouth.

A throbbing began deep in her stomach, radiating downward. A clock ticked somewhere in the room. Heavy breathing rent the air. Were the moans coming from her or Tyler? She couldn't tell. Their lips were seared together. She felt his heart pounding, racing faster. His hands slid down and gripped her hips, fitting her contours to his.

Fire lit in her belly and below. She couldn't have stopped, even if she wanted to. Which she didn't. She wanted him, needed him. The intensity of the past twenty-four hours erupted into overpowering passion.

She inhaled the unique scent that was Tyler's. Her legs wobbled. She clasped her hands behind his neck.

He broke the kiss, and she gave a cry of protest.

He lifted her in his arms, and he flicked his tongue

against the side of her neck, then circled the inside of her ear.

Her body had turned to a quivering mass of want. With great skill, he continued to seduce her. She clung to him desperately, pushing away the doubts, the fear, the anger.

"The time's right, now, babe," he murmured.

"Mmmm," was all she could manage. She lay heavily in his arms as he carried her to his bedroom.

He laid her on the bed, his body covering hers. Without giving her a chance to think about what they were doing, he began to lave her body with his tongue.

Her shirt came off. A cool breeze from the air conditioner brought goose bumps to her skin.

Or was it Tyler's lips, kissing their way down to her waist, teasing her with the fulfillment she craved?

She touched him, felt the bulge of his arousal. She began to quiver with the need to feel him inside her. She reached for his zipper, but his hand stopped her.

"Wait." He rolled to the side of the bed and stood. He removed his shirt, tossing it to the floor, then peeled off his jeans and shorts. He opened a drawer on the nightstand, removed something, and turned to face her.

She couldn't tear her gaze from his bronzed body and the proof of his desire jutting before him. She stretched out her arm and took a small packet from his fingers. "Let me."

When she'd finished sheathing him, he brushed the hair from her face and kissed her cheeks, her eyes, her chin. Then he moved down, down, stopping at her waist. Her mind screamed, "Don't stop."

"Slow and easy, babe," he murmured. He continued the sweet torture.

She couldn't bear much more without losing control.

His fingers loosened her jeans and moved them down her hips, his lips following, blowing warmly against her sensitive skin.

"Yes." She cried out, arching her body toward him.

When he finally pushed inside her, she screamed from the intense pleasure, clasping her legs around his waist.

Tyler delivered everything he promised, bringing her to an explosive climax. Then, he continued a sweet invasion of her body until they both exploded into an inferno of fire.

****

Tyler snuggled Grace closer against his chest. Her soft hair tickled against his skin. He'd known their lovemaking would be good, but he'd never imagined it would be so consuming. She'd taken as much as he took, given as much as he gave. His equal in every way. In his heart, he knew they'd shared more than sex.

He couldn't remember why he'd kissed Grace. One minute she'd been looking at him with daggers in her eyes, the next he was scooping her up and carrying her to bed.

Now she slept curled against him. He held her close until she began to stir, making his body hum again. All his senses seemed to gather forces in the tightening of his groin.

He felt her smile against his neck, her teeth making light contact, her fingers trailing softly against his chest.

"Mmm," she murmured, her breath hot against him.

The rhythm of his heart picked up speed, urging him to make her tremble beneath him again.

He kissed her eyelids, her nose, then captured her soft, willing lips. His hand reached back toward the nightstand, seeking another foil packet.

She opened her mouth, drawing his tongue inside.

He groaned and rolled her on top of him.

Her eyes, dark blue orbits of desire, met his gaze under half-closed lids. He touched her breast, marveling at the quickness of her response. Her nipples pebbled and she threw back her head, thrusting her chest against his hands.

He bent to pull one into his mouth when he felt

someone else's presence. He pushed himself away from her.

Grace groaned a protest.

Their gazes brushed. Then he looked toward the opened bedroom door and into the amused face of Jake Scott.

What the hell?

Tyler groaned, rolled to his side and pulled the sheet up to cover Grace.

"What are you doing here?" Tyler demanded.

Jake said, "Looks like I caught you at a bad time. Ms. Wilkins, I presume?"

Tyler looked down at Grace, surprised to see a grin on her face.

"Ah, hell. Grace, meet Jake Scott. Jake, Grace Wilkins."

Jake's lips tilted upward. "Nice to meet you, Grace." He gestured toward the living room. "I'll just wait out here while you finish...whatever you were—"

Tyler flung a pillow at his head. "Go to hell, Jake."

"Nice to meet you," Grace called out to Jake's back.

Tyler growled, kissed Grace with a promise that they would finish what they'd started, then sat on the side of the bed and reached for his jeans.

"Why do you suppose he's here?" Grace asked.

"I don't know, but I'm going to find out. I told him to send in some backup, but I didn't expect him to come." He stood and fastened his jeans, and then made the mistake of turning to look at Grace. She had pulled the sheet up to her neck, but the look in her eyes begged him to rip it off and continue what he'd started. "Hold that thought." He winked before closing the door.

Chapter Twelve

Jake sat on the sofa and propped his feet on the coffee table. "Nice digs."

"I asked what the hell you're doing here."

Jake motioned to the chair. "You called, remember? Sit down."

Tyler sank into the chair. "I asked for guys to do some surveillance."

"What, I don't qualify?"

Tyler ran a hand through his hair. "Things have been heating up."

"Obviously," Jake answered.

Tyler met Jake's amused glance.

"That's not what I meant."

Jake pulled his feet to the floor and leaned forward. "I've got news. Max is walking around with a new face."

"Just like we figured."

"Right. We've got the doc who did it."

"Couldn't you have told me this over the phone?"

"Yeah, but I thought you might want this, and you don't have a fax."

Jake held out a picture. Tyler recognized Max's eyes in the unfamiliar face.

"The 'after' picture. The doctor had a hidden camera. Felt he needed to protect himself."

A soft indrawn breath drew both men's attention to Grace. "I've seen that guy. If that's Max, he *is* here."

Tyler handed the picture to Grace. "Are you sure?"

"I'm positive. I know his eyes. I should have figured it out before now." She handed the picture back to Tyler. "I saw him outside the D.A.'s office when I returned my key. He watched me get on the elevator. Something about him seemed familiar. He gave me the creeps."

"I take it she knows?" Jake asked.

Grace swung to face him. "Don't talk as if I'm invisible. I know you sent Tyler here to find Max, and I know he's using me to do it. So, yes, I know."

Tyler put a hand on her waist. "Grace—"

She pushed his hand away. "I also know that you need my help if you want to succeed. So, whatever plans you have in mind better include me." She looked at Tyler, then at Jake. "Gentlemen, shall we talk?"

Jake held out his hand. "I'm glad to meet you, Grace, and I think you're right. We need to work together—"

"Not on your life," Tyler said. "We're not putting her in danger. This is our fight, not hers."

"You're wrong." Grace placed her hands on her hips. "This is *my* fight. Max is here for one reason. He wants me. You're here because you want Max. I'm the common denominator."

"She's right, Tyler. We need her."

This wasn't what Tyler wanted. Not now. Hadn't he and Grace moved to a new level in their relationship? How could he let her become a pawn in this game of revenge? He ran a hand through his hair and cursed under his breath.

****

Max waited until the old man and his gaudy companion drove away before leaving his hiding place. Something was up. He'd watched the two men on the porch talking as if plotting something, but he'd come too far to let anything stop him now.

Stupidity couldn't defeat genius. He'd show them no one could cross Max Clayton.

He slipped a tool from his pocket, inserted it in the lock, and opened the door of the old man's house. He walked into a small living room and gave it a quick once-over. A natural stone fireplace dominated one wall. The whole place had a rustic look, complimented by the heavy wood sofa with blue and brown plaid cushions, wood table lamps, hardwood floors with braided rugs in shades of brown, and a solid blue recliner. A mirror hung above the narrow mantle. Several pictures in wooden frames standing on the mantle were the only decorations. He lifted a picture frame and looked at a young woman's face, lips lifted in a smile, eyes sparkling as if hiding a happy secret. Her shoulder length brown hair parted in the middle and brushed her cheeks in soft waves. Who was she? The old man's daughter? Nice looking broad.

Max sat the picture back in place and moved into the kitchen. He removed the bag from his back, unzipped it and reached inside. In the past, he'd always assigned this type of job to one of his minions. Now he was reduced to doing his own dirty work. The only redeeming factor lay in knowing he'd soon have his revenge on Grace.

The bitch deserved every exciting thing he planned for her. All the previous kills only fueled his desire to save Grace for last. She knew the truth now—that Max had found her and her days were short on this earth. She'd turned against him, testified against him after all he'd done to make her life better. When he met her she was nothing but a cocktail waitress. He showered her with gifts, put her in a nicer apartment, introduced her to his friends and planned to marry her one day. Oh, yes, she deserved to die begging for her life.

His fingers deftly went to work. In a few minutes, he'd rigged the kitchen door to explode when it opened. Max checked the C-4 and the wiring to ensure it would ignite properly. He used a small charge, for he didn't want to set the entire mountainside on fire. He needed just enough to do major damage to the old man.

When Max was satisfied with his work, he closed the bag, shifted it onto his back and left the way he'd entered.

****

Grace looked at Jake. "What do you want me to do?"

"Why don't you tell me what you know about Max. Then we can put our heads together and come up with a plan."

"I don't like this," Tyler said. "Max is dangerous. I don't want—"

A loud explosion rent the air.

"Stay here," Tyler ordered, shoving Grace into the chair.

Anger brought her to her feet.

Tyler rushed toward the kitchen.

Jake followed closely behind. "What the hell?"

"Sounded like a bomb," Tyler said.

"Hurry," Grace said as she passed them both with a burst of speed, racing onto the deck.

"Grace, stay here until we find out what's going on."

"Not on your life," she cried, racing down the stairs.

Dark smoke rose above the tree line.

"Oh, my God, it looks like Brad's house," Grace yelled.

Sirens cut through the sounds of heavy breathing as she raced along the mountain toward her friend's house. She prayed she was wrong. Maybe someone had set fire to a heap of trash and it got out of control. But the explosion? Please, God, let it be anything but what her heart feared.

False hopes were quickly destroyed when they reached Brad's yard. He lay on the ground, his leg askew, his face and hands covered with black char. A small piece of wood protruded from his cheek. Large splinter-like spikes of wood peppered his arms.

Brightly colored clothes decorated the lawn, probably the ones Harri had intended for the church. The back porch had been destroyed and flames flickered along the outside wall of the kitchen. Grace registered everything within seconds, full of anger at the destruction. She looked around. Where was Harri?

She dropped to the ground beside Brad.

"Don't touch him," Tyler warned unnecessarily. He knelt on the ground and placed two fingers gently on Brad's neck. "He's alive."

Jake flipped open a cell phone and walked a few feet

away. She hoped he was calling an ambulance.

Grace leaned close to Brad's ear. "Brad, it's me. I'm here. Can you hear me?" Grace pleaded.

A car door slammed and Harri came running to where Brad lay. "Oh, no. Oh, no." Her eyes overflowed with tears. A low moan rose from her throat, then built to a loud, keening wail. "Brad!" She threw herself on him, but Tyler reacted quickly, lifting her off his prone body.

"Let me go." Harri struggled to break free, but Tyler kept her firmly in his grip.

"Harri, listen to me. Help is on the way. He might have broken bones. You don't want to hurt him any more than he already is, do you?"

Harri shook her head in defeat. Tyler awkwardly hugged her, continuing to assure her Brad would be all right. He looked over his shoulder at Grace.

"He's not responding," Grace said.

"He can't hear you right now. The blast will have deafened him temporarily."

A fire engine arrived, followed by an ambulance. Two paramedics pushed Grace back so they could tend to Brad. They examined him, attached an oxygen mask to his face, then lifted him onto a stretcher. Harri climbed into the ambulance and Grace tried to follow.

"There isn't room for both of you." The paramedic attending Brad gave her a sympathetic look and reached to close the door.

"I'll make room," Grace insisted. Her face must have shown her determination, for he offered no further argument as she squeezed in beside Harri.

He shut the door and the ambulance sped away, siren blaring. Grace and Harri were jostled from side to side, but Harri seemed unaffected. Black mascara ran unheeded down her cheeks. Her green tank top was smudged with the black smoke that riddled Brad's clothes and body.

Brad's eyes fluttered open and locked on Harri's face. "What...?" He grimaced in pain, then closed his eyes, losing consciousness.

"Brad, don't you dare give up," Grace ordered. "You're going to make it, you hear me? I need you. Harri needs you. Hang on. Please, please hang on."

Harri's fingers gently touched Brad's blackened fingers. "Brad, I love you so much. Please, don't leave me."

Grace leaned forward and looked at the ambulance driver. "Can't you go any faster?"

"No ma'am," he drawled.

The paramedic across from them pulled the stethoscope from his ears, letting it dangle around his neck. "He's going to make it. His heart is strong and his blood pressure is stable. None of his injuries seem life-threatening."

Grace clung to his words, grasping hope. She squeezed Harri's hand.

Harri turned her ravaged face to meet Grace's eyes. "This is my fault. I should have made him listen."

"Harri, it's not—"

"It's my fault. I told him I'd seen him lying in a hospital bed, but he laughed at me like he always does. He said he was perfectly healthy, that there wasn't a thing wrong with him. He wouldn't listen to me. We...we had an argument, and I dropped him off at the bottom of the drive and made him walk up the hill. He had to carry a box of clothes I'm donating for the church rummage sale, too. I should have driven him up here. Stayed with him."

"It's not your fault, Harri. Besides, those clothes probably kept him from being hurt more than he is. You didn't do anything to cause this. If you'd been with him, you'd have been hurt, too."

The ambulance pulled up to the emergency entrance at the hospital. The doors flew open and two attendants lifted Brad's stretcher. They pushed him through the automatic doors, and Grace and Harri followed closely behind.

While they rushed Brad away, Grace and Harri were

told to stay in the waiting room.

"Grace." She turned at the sound of her name.

Tyler walked up to them. "How's Brad?" he asked.

"We don't know anything yet." She flicked a glance at Harri, who sat stunned in one of the well-worn chairs.

"He's going to be okay," he assured them.

"Where's Jake?" Grace asked.

"I left him at Brad's place talking to the sheriff."

Tyler brushed a lock of hair off her forehead.

It seemed hours before a doctor finally approached them. "Which one of you is Harri?" he asked.

Harri jumped up. "I am."

"He's awake and asking to see you. You can visit for a few minutes. One caution, he won't be able to hear you clearly right now."

"But how is he otherwise?" Grace asked.

The doctor turned to her. "Are you a relative?"

Grace hesitated for a second before replying. "I'm his granddaughter."

The doctor smiled at her. "Your grandfather's leg is broken in two places. He'll be in a cast for a while. He's a fairly healthy man for his age. He has a few burns and cuts, bruised ribs. It could have been worse. We'll keep him in the recovery room until he stabilizes. Only one person at a time can see him until we move him into a room. In the meantime, someone needs to fill out paperwork so we can admit him."

"I'll take care of that," Tyler spoke up. Grace gave him a grateful smile. The doctor led Harri away and Tyler went to the admitting desk.

Left alone, Grace felt her earlier fears fade with a growing anger. She sat dry-eyed, chewing on the inside of her cheek, using the pain to keep her from running off to find Max.

The man was evil through and through. She couldn't imagine what demons drove him. How had she ever found him attractive?

He deserved to die. Look at all the innocent lives he'd

destroyed by smuggling in billions of dollars worth of street drugs. She shuddered, knowing she'd nearly become one of his 'girls.'

Though she'd escaped, she still felt tainted. Now he'd brought his dirty games to Foxfire, hoping to destroy her and those she loved. It was time she stood up to him. Time to stop his evil reach.

He wanted to kill her?

She'd give him the opportunity.

But it would be Max who died.

****

Grace had never seen Brad look so vulnerable. To her, he'd always been vital, full of life. He'd been moved to a private room Tyler had arranged. His eyes were closed, his face pale. A cast covered his leg from ankle to thigh, and a monitor beeped steadily at the head of his bed.

Harri sat in a chair next to the bed, her hand lying gently on his.

Tyler came into the room, glanced at Harri, then moved to Grace's side. She had to find a way to get rid of him without making him suspicious. She glanced out the window at the sun's orange glow. Soon it would drop below the horizon and Grace wanted to be back in Foxfire before dark.

Tyler leaned close and asked in a hushed voice, "Are you ready to leave?"

"I'm going to stay here. I don't want to leave him."

"The doctor said he'd sleep through the night. There's nothing you can do by staying. You need to rest, too." He touched her shoulder. "Don't forget about Tiffany."

Just like Tyler to use her dog as a bribe. However, if she didn't deal with Max tonight, other innocent people would be hurt. "That's unfair," she responded sharply.

He paced to the door and back, his hand combing through his hair. He stopped beside her chair. "You're right. I'm just worried about you."

Looking into his concerned gaze, she almost believed him. Almost.

"Where's Jake?" she asked.

"He went back to the apartment to check on some leads. With all his resources, we're bound to catch Max before long. I told him we'd be joining him soon."

"I think I'd rather sleep at my house," Grace said. "That way you two can work without any distraction."

Tyler frowned and nodded toward the hallway.

Grace glanced at Harri, who appeared to be listening intently to their conversation. Deciding not to upset her further, Grace followed Tyler out of the room.

His face showed stress from the last two days. Shadows ringed his eyes, making them appear more deep-set. Stubble dotted his jaw line which only emphasized the tired lines etching his face. Even his voice sounded tired as he spoke. "What happened to your big speech about being included in our plans? Did you change your mind? Not that I'm complaining."

"I'm just worn out mentally," Grace said. "I don't think I'd be any help tonight at all."

"You need someplace safe to sleep. Come home with me. You can have the bedroom. Jake and I can camp out in the living room."

She gazed into his eyes, knowing he would never agree to let her stay alone. Not until Max was caught. "I want to stay a little longer. When Adam comes back from the cafeteria, he can drive us to Harri's house and I'll spend the night with her. She shouldn't be alone either." She must have sounded convincing for she saw the tension easing from his face.

"That's a good idea. I'll send a couple of men to watch the house just in case. You'll probably be safer at Harri's anyway. I'll wait for Adam to make sure he doesn't mind."

"You don't have to wait. He has to drive back anyway. I'm sure he won't mind. He'll be going right past Harri's. Why don't you go ahead. You look tired, too. I'll call when we get there."

"I don't want to leave you alone."

"I'm not alone. There's a bodyguard at the door,

thanks to you."

He pushed away from the wall. "Watch for anything that looks or sounds suspicious. Max is out there somewhere." His unspoken words hung heavy between them. *Max would be looking for her.*

Grace was counting on it. Tyler talked to the man guarding Mike's room and held the door open for her. She went back inside, and the door closed softly behind her.

"Where's Tyler?" Harri asked.

She felt bad lying to Harri, but there was no other option. She had to protect her friends. "He went outside to use his cell phone. He's waiting for me. Are you going to stay here tonight or should I ask Adam to drive you home?"

"I'm not leaving Brad's side." Her worried glance went back to Brad.

Grace hugged her. "He's going to be fine, you know. Don't worry."

Harri wiped a tear from her face. "I can't help worrying. I love him."

"Me, too." Grace leaned down and kissed Brad's cheek. "I love you," she said. Grace wished she could reassure him there'd be no further danger. She owed him that much and more.

Grace hugged Harri again before she left. There was a strong possibility she'd never see her friends again. Though she knew she had no choice but to face Max, in all reality he might kill her. For all her bravado, she wasn't certain she could best him. Sure, she'd had her self-defense classes, but would she even remember what to do? Knowing ahead of time what the attacker would do worked well in a classroom setting, but in reality, one never knew what might happen.

She had her gun, but even Tyler doubted she could shoot anyone. Could she? If faced with life or death, could she pull the trigger? All she could do was pray her strength held out and she actually got a chance to face that dilemma. Odds were against her. Still she had no choice.

The elevator doors opened and Grace stepped into the hospital lobby and gazed around to make sure Tyler was nowhere in sight. She walked over to the information desk. Grace explained about riding to the hospital in the ambulance and forgetting to bring her purse. She asked if the woman would call her a cab and went outside to wait.

She paced the small sidewalk outside the main entrance, getting more nervous as the minutes ticked slowly by. Just when she decided to go back inside and ask the woman to call again, a cab pulled up. Heaving a sigh of relief, she climbed into the back and gave the driver her address.

"Lady, that's at least thirty miles. Do you know how expensive this is going to be?"

"I know. Don't worry about the money. I'll pay you."

He shrugged and pulled away from the hospital.

She settled into the seat. Her attention was drawn to the back of the driver's head. Something about him seemed familiar. She darted a glance at the rear view mirror, but he had a cap pulled over his forehead, shadowing his face. Her heart jumped. Could it be Max? Impossible. How would he know she'd call a cab?

She closed her eyes and leaned her head back. Foolish. Her imagination was running away with her. She dried her clammy hands on her jeans and sneaked another look at the driver. Though she couldn't see his eyes, she knew he was looking at her, too.

The cab continued moving on a correct route to her house. Max wouldn't drive her home. He'd take her off some place and kill her.

She battled her overactive imagination as the sun dropped below the horizon. It was fully dark when they pulled into her driveway forty minutes later. She asked the driver to wait while she went inside to get his fare.

He nodded without speaking.

She kept her back straight and tried not to run. At any moment she expected a bullet to take her down. She ventured a look back before she opened the door and slipped inside. She closed the door and peered through the peephole. She flipped on the porch light as he stepped out of the cab and leaned a hip against it, staring at the house.

The driver wasn't Max. She'd never seen this man before. She shook off her tension and hurried to get her purse.

After she paid him, he thanked her, gave her a half-hearted smile, and drove off. She watched the taillights disappear before she turned and went back inside.

Chapter Thirteen

Tyler dialed Harri's number and put the phone to his ear. Why hadn't Grace called yet?

"Give it a rest. You called less than five minutes ago," Jake said.

"Something's wrong." Tyler glanced at his watch. "They should be there by now."

"Maybe they stopped to eat. It's been a long day for everyone."

"Maybe." Tyler closed the phone. It was a possibility, but Tyler had a bad feeling chewing at his gut. "I'll give them another half-hour, but if she doesn't call by eight, I'm heading back to the hospital. It would be just like her and Harri to stay the night with Brad."

"So? We've got a man there."

"You know as well as I do there are no guarantees. Max is full of surprises. I want Grace here where I can protect her."

Jake laughed. "Is that what you were doing when I got here today? Keeping her safe?"

"That's none of your business."

"Natalie's been gone a long time, Tyler. I loved her, too. But you need to move on. Get over it. Grace seems like a woman who has her head on straight." He grinned wickedly. "The rest isn't bad either."

"Don't go there, Jake."

Jake held up his hands. "I'm not planning to move in on your territory, but do yourself a favor and admit you're in love with her."

He wasn't in love with her. He'd admit he felt something...but love? He doubted he'd ever love anyone again. He was too jaded. Yet, he did long to have what his dad and mom had. Their relationship had been solid and strong until the day she died.

Tyler had thought Natalie and he had that kind of relationship, until Max had destroyed that dream. That's why Tyler had to forget how Grace felt in his arms, how she tasted, how she moved when—

"I'm not admitting anything," Tyler said. "We have a job to do."

"Any leads?"

"Nothing in the hotels or motels angle. If he's still around, he's got to be holed up in a vacant house. I can't see Max camping in the woods. He's not the type."

"You're right. My gut tells me he's close by. I just don't know the area good enough to scout him out. We need Grace's help." He looked at his watch. "Damn it. Where is she? Did you send a guy to Harri's?"

"I asked Rob to fly in, but he's not here yet. I told him to take a cab. He's got the address. He'll call when he lands and I'll tell him to report back once he gets to Harri's place."

Tyler paced to the kitchen and back bringing a bag of chips. He plopped in the chair and dropped the bag on the coffee table. "Damn. A bomb. How the hell did Max manage that?"

"Easy. We found some traces of C-4. He's no dummy. He rigged it to blow but used just enough to make it a small blast. But why did he target the old man?"

"Because he means so much to Grace. This whole thing is about retribution. He's getting even, but since he and Grace were once an item, he wants to make sure she suffers. No quick kill for her. It's all about power, control, and getting even."

****

Grace went into her darkened house, leaving the door unlocked. She wanted no obstacles for Max. Her plan was simple. She'd wait for him in her bedroom. Max would expect her to be upset over Brad. He should remember that she became a tiger when backed against a wall. She'd defeated him once, and she'd do it again. When he came after her, she'd pull the gun from under her pillow and shoot him between the eyes.

Her plan had just one flaw. If she turned on the lights, Tyler would know she was home, but if she didn't, Max wouldn't.

Tyler would make her stay at his place or insist on staying here with her. If she didn't set herself up to lure Max in tonight, he'd strike out against someone else she loved. Tyler might think he could outsmart Max, but Grace couldn't take that chance. She picked up the phone and dialed Tyler's number.

"Grace, what took so long?" Tyler's voice told her he'd been concerned. "Where are you?"

"I'm...we're at Harri's. It took a while to convince her to leave Brad. I'm sorry if you were worried."

"Damn right I was worried. I was ready to come to the hospital and drag you both out."

"I said I was sorry. It couldn't be helped. She wanted to make sure he'd stay asleep through the night. She loves him." She took a quick breath. "How's Tiffany?" She could picture Tyler's hand messing his hair in frustration.

"She's fine. I fed her and she ate every bite. Tomorrow we'll take her outside and let her get some strength back in her legs."

A stabbing pain clutched her chest. She hoped she had the chance to do that, but tomorrow she might be dead. She prayed not, for she wanted so much more. If her plan worked, Max would die in her place. She had to remain confident. She could defeat him. "Thank you."

"No problem. I'll swing by and pick you and Harri up in the morning. We can stop to see Brad. I know Harri will want to stay with him, but Jake and I need your help. We think Max is holed up in a vacant house. Can you think of any place he might be hiding?"

The cabin at Hannah Falls was the only vacant place on this side of the mountain. If he was staying close, that's where he'd be. Maybe he'd been there all along.

She'd thought Adam had followed her and Tyler to Hannah Falls that day, but maybe it hadn't been him. Maybe it had been Max. "I can't think straight tonight. Right now all I want is a hot shower and bed."

"Okay, babe. Get some rest. We'll talk in the morning. Can you put Harri on the phone for a minute?"

For a moment Grace panicked. "Um, Harri's in the shower right now." She hated the lies. Hadn't she been upset with him for his deception? She'd held it against him, even though she was as guilty as he for keeping secrets and telling lies. But she was doing it to protect him. A pain twisted her heart. And he'd been doing it to protect her. If she lived through the night, she'd tell him the truth. That she loved him. That she wanted him in her life.

He paused for a second, then said, "Make sure everything is locked up before you go to bed."

Grace breathed a quiet sigh of relief. He believed her. "I did that as soon as we got here." She exaggerated a yawn.

"You and Harri get a good night's rest. Call if you see or hear anything suspicious. We're sending a man over to watch the house, but his plane hasn't landed yet. I think you'll be safe enough. I doubt Max knows where Harri lives."

"I'm sure you're right. Goodbye, Tyler." She might be saying goodbye forever. She'd might never hear his voice again, never see his face or feel his arms around her. A gnawing ache settled in her chest. After making love with Tyler, she knew without a doubt that she loved him with all her heart. The realization of all she might lose slapped her hard, making her throat tighten and her eyes smart with unwanted tears. She had to stop thinking about it. She couldn't afford to be caught up in these feelings. Not if she had any chance of stopping Max. She had to be strong, and confident, and ready.

She hung up and went into the bedroom to retrieve her gun. She turned on the bedside lamp and opened the drawer on the nightstand. Her heart rate doubled when she saw the gun was missing. In its place was the necklace Max had given her in her other lifetime.

"Is this what you're looking for?"

She didn't have to see him to know Max was behind her.

"We meet again, Gracie Jo."

"Don't call me that."

Her eyes frantically searched for a weapon, but there was nothing except the lamp. She slowly stretched her arm toward it.

"Don't even think about it," Max said.

She straightened and turned to face her nemesis. He stood in front of the closet, holding her gun in his hand.

"What do you want, Max?" she asked.

He gave a short brittle laugh. "So you recognize me? What do you think of my new face?"

"It matches the ugliness inside you. What do you want?"

"I want a lot of things." His eyes turned feral, his glance narrowing in on hers. "I want you to put on the necklace, Gracie Jo."

"No."

He pointed the gun at her.

"You won't shoot me. If you do, people will come running. You can't afford to take the chance. They're on to you, you know." She took a step forward, trying to bluff him with a confidence she didn't trust.

"Ah, but I don't need to shoot you." With his free hand, he flipped open a long lethal-looking knife. "Now put on the necklace like a good girl."

Her chest threatened to explode with fear. She prayed it didn't show in her eyes. The last thing she wanted was for him to see he frightened her.

"I'll scream if you come one step closer."

"This knife will be buried in your heart before the first sound escapes your throat." His lips pulled upward in a grin that never reached his rat-like eyes. "I said, put the necklace on."

Grace's hand fumbled in the drawer until she touched the cool stones. She closed her fingers around the necklace and threw it at him. She started to run, but he moved sideways, blocking her exit. She froze. He tossed the gun on the bed. Sweat trickled down her armpits, though her body chilled as if her blood had been iced. The knife kept her attention. She was afraid to look away. Afraid he'd carry through with his threat.

She glanced at the bed from the corner of her eye. The gun was close, but not quite close enough. She clutched her hands into fists, then opened the fingers slowly, willing the blood to warm them.

He picked up the necklace. "Come on, honey." He held his open palm up, the heavy necklace draping over it. "You don't want it?" He shoved it in his pocket. "Probably for the best. It would just get in the way." He nodded toward the gun. "I'm giving you a chance. Let's see who's the fastest."

She read the insanity in his eyes. Her arms felt like lead, while her knees threatened to buckle. She lifted her chin a notch higher. "Like you gave my dog a chance?"

He rubbed the blunt side of the knife along his nose. "Ah, the dog. Most unfortunate. I've always liked dogs."

Every muscle in her body screamed for her to lunge for the gun and blast his taunting face away. "You're a cruel bastard."

His eyebrows raised in mock surprise. "Me? You call me cruel, when you disfigured me, then tried to destroy me with your testimony?"

His voice, no longer controlled, boomed through her tiny bedroom. "Do you know how much trouble you caused me? Do you even care?"

"Why should I care? Look what you did to me."

"All I did was offer you a job where you could make a lot of money."

"Offer? Hardly. You kidnapped me and forced me to—"

"The way I remember it, you came to me willingly. You liked what I had to offer. And you paid me back by destroying my looks. Just like I'm going to destroy yours. Maybe I won't kill you after all. Maybe I'll just carve you up so bad no man will ever look at you again." He moved a step closer. "Before I do, do you want to go at it for old time's sake?"

If she could keep him talking, she might be able to get away. She inched her foot closer to the bed.

"You deserved what I did to you, Max. I thought you loved me, but you were only using me. What was I? A trophy?"

"I would have married you. But you left me. You betrayed me."

"Only after you tried to make me one of your prostitutes. You disgust me. What excuse do you have for hurting Brad? He didn't do a damn thing to you."

"Brad?" Max touched the tip of the knife to his chin. "Ah, the old man. Were you sleeping with him, too?"

How dare he? She wanted to feel his face cave against her bare hands. Wanted to hear bones crunch. Wanted to dig her fingers into his scrawny neck and choke the life from him. She raised her fists.

"Angry, are you? Hmmm. I've got the knife and you've got...a gun if you're clever enough to get it. Why don't you try? Don't you want to shoot me? Or are you afraid?" He waved the knife in front of his face. "Does this scare you? What if I carved your face a little bit? Just a small teaser of things to come? Once I've finished with you do you think that vet will still want to screw you?"

A thousand spiders crawled up her spine. What were the chances of her reaching the gun in time? If she dove for the bed and rolled, she'd be a moving target, but she had to try.

With a burst of confidence, she threw herself toward the bed and grabbed the gun. She rolled, holding it in two hands, her finger on the trigger, and met his feral eyes gleaming like the blade of steel resting against her throat.

Chapter Fourteen

Tyler snapped his fingers. "Adam. How did I forget about him? He's familiar with everything and everyone in Foxfire. If there's a vacant house, he'll know about it." He grabbed the telephone book and began scanning the names.

"Will he help us?" Jake asked, leaning over Tyler's shoulder.

"Yeah." Tyler found the number and dialed. Adam answered on the second ring.

"Adam. This is Tyler. Listen, I need your help. Are there any vacant houses in Foxfire?"

"You wanting to rent a place for your friend?" Adam sounded puzzled.

Since the sheriff knew Tyler worked for Jake, Tyler supposed by now that Adam knew, too. He might appear a bit dim-witted, but nothing transpired in Foxfire without his knowledge. Tyler's undercover days were over. Once Max was caught, Tyler could spend the rest of his life doing what he loved—taking care of animals and loving Grace. It was all within his reach. "No, I'm looking for a place someone might hole up if they didn't want to be found."

Adam's voice lifted in boyish excitement. "You think that serial killer is hiding in Foxfire? I knew it! I've been trying to tell Brad, but he wouldn't listen. And look what happened to him. Are you going to make me a special deputy or something?"

Tyler grinned despite himself. "I would if I could, Adam, but I'm not a cop. However, you are the resident expert."

"Do you want me to come down and we can

170

brainstorm? I think I've got a map around here someplace."

Tyler lifted his hand, thumb and forefinger joined in a circle of success. He grinned at Jake. "That would be a big help, Adam. See you in a bit." He hung up.

"I wish it was still light outside. Even though Adam knows these hills, we'll probably give ourselves away tromping through unknown territory. We may have to wait until morning after all."

Jake's phone rang. He put it to his ear and answered. A frown crossed his face. "You're sure?"

"Who is it?" Tyler asked.

Jake turned his back. "Okay. How much time can you buy?"

Another pause. Tyler could tell something big was coming down. Adrenalin flushed his veins, and his stomach tightened in anticipation, just as it always did when his target was in sight. Soon he'd have the satisfaction of avenging Natalie's death. Would he then be able to put aside his guilt and find love again? Did he have a chance with Grace? Did he really want to find out?

Jake hung up and faced Tyler. "You didn't tell me there was a serial killer operating here."

"What does that have to do with catching Max?"

"They lifted some prints from Brad's house. They match with Max's."

"So what? We knew Max did that."

"And they checked Max's DNA to that found on the victims of the Knoxville Knifer. That matches, too."

"Holy crap.

****

Adam backed his truck onto the road and headed for Tyler's house. He was flattered that Tyler called him. Most people thought of him as a backwoods hillbilly. Now he had a chance to show them he had a lot more brains than they gave him credit for. He saw a light on at Grace's house and thought about stopping to tell her the news. But that wouldn't do. He should tell Lainey first.

Even as the thought crossed his mind, he turned into Grace's drive. He could use the excuse that he wanted to find out if she had any news about Brad. He'd tell her about Tyler wanting his help, and then he could mention that he thought the killer might be holed up in that old cabin above the falls. Maybe he and Grace could go after the killer themselves. Wouldn't that be the cat's pajamas? They'd have their pictures taken and be on the front page of the newspaper, just like her and that attorney guy. Yessir, people would look up to him after that.

He parked the truck, jogged to her front door and knocked. He called out and knocked again, then walked around to the back when he didn't get a response. Funny, her lights were on. She should be inside. He put his hands on the window and peered inside. He didn't see or hear anything.

Harri had said Grace left with Tyler. Maybe she was still with him. He'd better just drive on down and forget about catching the killer by himself.

Disheartened, he walked back to his truck and opened the door. As he slipped behind the wheel, he noticed a light bobbing through the trees beside the path.

The only people who lived on this section of the mountain were Brad, Grace, Tyler and himself. Who could be walking through the woods this time of night?

A chill crept across his scalp, making it feel as if his hair stood on end beneath the ball cap. Maybe the Knoxville Knifer was out there. He couldn't take a chance on letting him get away. He couldn't waste time driving down to the clinic.

He quietly shut the truck door and started the engine. He had to get his rifle. And he'd call Tyler. But he'd be the first one to catch up with the perp. He liked that term. TV cops used it all the time.

Tonight he'd become a hero.

****

Tyler went down to the clinic to close up and turn off the lights. This time Jake accompanied him.

"So this is where you plan to spend your time from now on, huh?"

"Yes. And I think I can convince Dad to join me."

Jake clapped him on the shoulder. "I hope so. You deserve a new start. Natalie would want that."

"You're right. She would. You know I loved her with all my heart."

"I know. She loved you back. But she's gone. Nothing can change that. All we can do is bring her killer to justice. Then I'll be able to sleep at night."

"Me, too."

"I don't think you'll get much sleep if Grace has anything to do with it," Jake quipped.

"I sure hope not."

They laughed. Jake tilted his head. "Is that a phone ringing?"

Tyler listened but didn't hear anything. "It might have been my cell. I left it upstairs."

They climbed the stairs to the apartment and Tyler checked his phone. He had one message.

****

Adam knew the killer was headed for Hannah Falls, since the light kept moving in that direction. The secluded cabin would make a perfect hiding place. When Tyler asked if Adam knew a vacant house, he'd immediately thought of his family cabin, long-ago abandoned. He'd planned to show Tyler and his friend where it was, but now Adam would have to go on his own. He'd left a message on Tyler's answering machine, but catching this guy would be up to Adam.

Once he caught the killer, he'd be hailed a hero. No one would call him "weird" Adam again. Oh, they didn't think he knew what they said behind his back, but he did. All his life, he'd been different. People laughed because he took responsibility for looking out for their welfare. Over the years, he'd been forced to sell off his family property, but he'd made sure he sold only to good people. Like Grace.

173

Grace would look at him differently after he captured this guy, too. She might even regret turning him down when he'd asked her out. He'd always have a soft spot for her, but Lainey was the best woman for him. Just knowing Grace would think of him as an equal would be enough to make him happy.

Yes, after tonight, he'd be a hero in everyone's eyes.

He shifted the heavy rifle, hoping it would be enough of a threat to capture the bad guy, because Adam didn't think he could actually fire the gun.

The last time he'd fired it, he'd been a teenager. His dad took him hunting. They spent hours in the cold damp morning air waiting for an unsuspecting deer. Adam hadn't wanted to go, but he didn't want to disappoint his dad. Unlike his grandfather, his dad thought Adam was a sissy. Adam hoped to prove him wrong by bringing home the biggest buck ever.

Finally, they were rewarded for their patience. A huge antlered buck came into the clearing. Adam took aim. The rifle butt jammed against his shoulder, bruising his bone. He looked down the barrel through the sight, focusing on his target.

"Careful," his dad whispered. "Steady does it."

Adam's lungs ached from the short shallow breaths he managed to take. Fear traveled through his veins. He and the buck stared at each other, into each other, and Adam's body quivered. He focused on keeping his rifle steady and not giving in to his niggling conscience.

He tightened his finger on the trigger.

"Now," his dad whispered. "Do it."

Adam sent a silent warning. *Run.*

The deer lunged off into the deep cover of the woods. Adam pulled the trigger. The bullet sped harmlessly into the treetops.

The force of the recoil knocked him to the ground. He pushed himself to his feet, waiting for his father's wrath. Instead of the anticipated anger, Adam read pity in his eyes. That stung him more fiercely than any words could have done.

His dad never invited him to go hunting again.

Adam hadn't considered using the rifle again until tonight. He didn't even know if it would fire, but he'd stuffed a cartridge in, just in case.

In the distance he heard a muffled shout. He swallowed hard. His destiny awaited him.

****

Adam's voice boomed from the phone. With each word, Tyler's apprehension grew.

"Tyler, I'm going to the cabin at Hannah Falls to catch the serial killer. He's heading that way. I saw him. Well, not him, but his light. That's the only place I know of he could hole up. I went by Grace's house. That's when I saw him, but Grace must be with you. When you get this message, she can show you the back road that goes to the cabin. It's faster. I'll hold him there until you come to get him."

"What the—?"

Tyler hit the replay button silencing Jake's question. They listened to Adam's message again.

Jake's penetrating gaze met Tyler's. "What the hell is he talking about? Where's Grace? I thought—"

"She lied to me. She didn't go to Harri's at all. She went home. And now Max has her."

"You don't know that for sure," Jake said.

"Trust me. I know."

"Do you know what cabin Adam was talking about?"

"Yeah. I don't know about a back road, but if it exists, I'll find it." He dialed the hospital. Just as he'd suspected Harri was still there.

"But I thought Grace went home with you. That's what she told me."

"Listen, Harri. We don't have much time. Max has her and he's taking her to the cabin at Hannah Falls. Adam says there's a back road. How do I find it?"

He listened to her directions and hung up the phone. "Let's go." Tyler tucked his gun in the waistband of his jeans. "If we don't beat Adam, Max will kill both of them."

Jake called for backup before climbing into the passenger seat of Tyler's pickup. "Let's get this show on the road," he said.

Tyler gunned the motor and sped onto the main road. They couldn't afford to waste any time. Not if he wanted to save Grace. His gut clenched in fear, fear of losing Grace. He loved her. He couldn't let history repeat itself. He couldn't lose her. He pressed his foot to the accelerator.

****

Grace pushed against the nauseating rag with her tongue, but it remained lodged in her mouth. She and Max had trekked most of the distance to Hannah Falls. She could hear the waterfall now. What good would it do if she did spit out the vile cloth? No one could hear her scream. Not that she'd resort to yelling for help. She had youth, stamina, and determination on her side. Though he had control at the moment, she'd gain the upper hand somehow.

All she had to do was free her hands. She'd tightened her fists before he knotted Tiffany's leather leash around her wrists. She'd been stretching the thin leather without Max's knowledge, while he walked beside her, pressing the gun against her spine. One of her wrists now slipped partially from the bond. She wiggled her fingers to start the blood flowing.

Max stumbled and righted himself. His heavy breathing worsened the farther they climbed. Inwardly, she smiled at his discomfort, while she forged ahead a little faster. He held the flashlight in one hand, lighting the trail, but she didn't need it to guide her. She'd hiked to Hannah Falls many times.

Max lurched sideways and let out a loud curse. He took a few limping steps and ordered her to stop. She considered running off the well-worn path into the dense woods. Max would never catch her. She could lead him aimlessly through the mountain for hours. But if he didn't chase her, he might escape. She couldn't risk it. This had to end tonight.

She turned to face him, watching him rub his ankle. He kept the gun pointed in her direction, but he placed the light on the ground. Grace moved her wrist a little further from the leather knot and suddenly she was free.

Not wasting a moment, she kicked out, catching Max by surprise and knocking the gun from his hand. Her next well-placed kick connected with his nose, sending him sprawling backwards.

He cursed and grabbed his face. The flashlight illuminated blood spurting between his fingers. "You stupid bitch."

She yanked the gag from her mouth and threw it to the ground.

He pushed to a sitting position and reached for the gun.

Grace dove for it. Her fingers closed around the weapon seconds before his hand gripped hers. They struggled for a few seconds, and then he wrested the gun from her. She saw the weapon coming and tried to move away, but she wasn't quick enough. A sharp pain echoed through her skull. She tasted dirt as his weight pinned her to the ground and forced the air from her lungs. Her ears filled with a loud ringing noise. Blinking her eyes caused an unbearable tightening band around her forehead.

"Bitch."

The pain in her head increased. Totally disoriented, she concentrated on gathering strength to dislodge him from her back.

"You broke my nose." His words sounded muffled and strange.

Light flashed behind her eyes and she gave in to the pressure that cracked her head like a fallen coconut.

Then everything turned black.

****

"Wake up, bitch."

A stinging slap made Grace lift her heavy eyelids. Where was she? A blinding light played across her face. She closed her eyes against the intrusion.

"Get up."

Someone tugged at her shoulders. She pushed at the offending hands.

"Damn it, I know you're awake. Now, get up."

An open palm connected loudly with her cheek, and everything came rushing back in a swirling barrage. Max had hit her with the gun. She pushed at the fog in her brain and tried to lift her eyelids.

Through shuttered eyes, she struggled to focus on Max's bloody face. Satisfaction crept over her, easing the throbbing pain in her head. She'd gotten in her licks. His nose job would need repair, if he lived, which Grace was determined wouldn't happen. She pushed to a sitting position, weaving drunkenly, swallowing back the bile rising in her throat.

Max grabbed her arm, yanking her to her feet. "Let's go."

He pushed her forward, not bothering to bind her arms. Big mistake for him to think she was too weak to overpower him.

Max's labored breathing fueled her confidence, and anger gave her strength, but the thump, thump, thump in her temples made it hard to concentrate. Why hadn't he killed her back at the house? Why was he taking her to the cabin?

She pushed a branch out of her way and released it.

Max cursed.

Score one for the good guys.

A light blinked through the trees. Had he left a light on in the cabin? Funny. She didn't remember it having electricity. She stepped into a clearing overgrown with kudzu. The ugly vines grew rampant through the mountains, covering everything in their path with a thick green blanket. She hadn't seen the cabin in years. It must be covered with the stuff. In the moonlight, she could see the outline of the rundown cabin. No light glowed behind the broken windowpanes. Had it been a reflection of the moon she'd seen, or a result of her head injury?

"Come on. Move." Max's words wheezed from his throat. He dug the gun into her spine.

She didn't want to find out what waited for her in the cabin. Her best chance of survival would be to strike while Max still struggled to catch his breath.

She threw herself to the ground, rolling to her back and catching Max by surprise. Drawing her knees to her chest she kicked out with both feet, landing a blow directly to Max's groin.

He crumpled, dropping the gun.

Pain slowed her as she looked around for the gun. Suddenly the clouds shifted and a shaft of moonlight glinted off the metal. She pushed to her knees and crawled toward it, but Max closed his hand around her ankle.

"No!" She kicked with her free foot, but his grip was like an iron cuff. She stretched her fingers toward the weapon.

"You're not going anywhere," he snarled, digging his fingers painfully into her ankle. "Not alive, anyway."

"I'm not going to die, Max. You are!" Her fingers touched the gun.

A soft click sounded.

The switchblade. How could she have forgotten about that?

"Move your hand away from the gun. Don't worry, *I'm* not going to kill you, Gracie Jo. You're going to be the next victim of the Knoxville Knifer."

He grabbed her hair. "Get up, Gracie Jo. Don't you want to look into the face of the notorious serial killer before you die?"

Max was the Knoxville Knifer? Pain became a burning inferno. Her scalp seemed to be ripping from her skull. She rose slowly. The trees and night sky swayed dizzily before she gained her balance.

Max's voice droned on. "By the time they find you, I'll be long gone. These rednecks will spend the next ten years looking for their serial killer, but they won't find him. All they'll find is you after the animals have fed on your dead flesh."

"You won't get away with this. The FBI knows you're here."

His grin froze her blood.

Grace shuddered. How many women had died because of her? How many did he kill to set up a cover for her murder?

The knife's point pricked her skin. A warm trickle of blood ran down her neck. This was it. She was going to die.

"Get away from her and drop the knife."

Her heart thudded. She raised her gaze and saw Adam standing several feet away, a rifle pointed at them.

Max gave a bitter laugh.

"I said drop the knife," Adam repeated. His voice shook and so did the rifle. Grace wondered if he knew how to shoot that thing. What if he panicked and shot her? What if he didn't shoot and Max killed both of them? Grace had to get the knife away from Max. She doubted Adam could ever pull the trigger. She had no doubt she was going to die, but she couldn't let Adam die, too.

"Grace, come over here," Adam said. "I've got him covered."

Max's arm tightened around her neck. "You crazy bastard, you'll never shoot," Max taunted.

The knife no longer pierced her skin. "He's a sharpshooter," Grace croaked. "I wouldn't tempt him if I were you." The knife moved away from her throat and his grip loosened.

"I'll have this knife plunged into her throat before your bullet gets here. You want to risk it?"

"I'll shoot if you don't let her go."

Taking advantage of the situation, Grace wrapped her leg around Max's and pulled, dropping toward the ground and bringing him with her. She hit hard with Max on top, driving the air from her lungs.

With a move faster than she'd anticipated, Max grabbed her hair, yanking her head up and pressing the knife beneath her chin.

She gave a cry of pain and fury.

Once more the knife pricked her skin.

"Drop the rifle or I'll slit her throat."

"No! Don't listen to him. Shoot him." She closed her eyes, willing Adam to pull the trigger.

"I can blow your head clean off from here," Adam shouted.

Max laughed. "Sure you can, Rambo."

"Do it." Grace felt the knife drawing blood. "Shoot him," she begged. "He's going to kill me anyway."

"He's not going to kill anybody." Tyler's voice boomed from the wooded area beside the cabin.

Tyler?

"Drop it, Max, or you're a dead man." Tyler's tone left no doubt he had faced danger before and come out the winner. Between the pain and the fear she'd forgotten that Tyler had come to Foxfire for one reason—to kill Max. This wasn't the flirtatious veterinarian she'd fallen in love with. This was the hard-core special investigator. The man sworn to bring down Max Clayton.

Max looked from Adam to Tyler. "What are you going to do? Shoot? Who do you think will catch the bullet, me or her? I don't think either of you will take the chance."

Max slowly moved to stand, keeping Grace clutched tightly against him. "Maybe I'll just finish her off now," he taunted. "Or maybe I'll just carve her up a little."

The sound of Adam cocking the rifle echoed through the clearing.

Grace's legs began to wobble. She had to do something. Tyler stepped closer and she sent him a message with her eyes, hoping he'd read her intent. She drove her elbow backward into Max's chest. He grunted and suddenly her arms were free.

"Bastard," she spat out. She reached for his wrist. He was stronger than she thought and he tugged on her hair again. She gasped, but kept her grip on his arm. The knife moved closer to her throat. Through force of will, she kept her grip on his arm, but pain exploded violently through her head. She wouldn't let him win. Dying wasn't an option.

The rifle blasted a second before another shot rang out.

She and Max fell to the ground.

Max was on top of her. She couldn't breathe. Had she been shot?

Suddenly Max's weight lifted.

"It's over, Grace." Tyler reached out his hand.

"Tyler!" she cried. Their fingers melded together and then his strong arms pulled her against him.

"I've got you, babe. You're safe now."

"Max?"

"He's not going anywhere."

She clung to him, heart beating rapidly, forgetting the pain ricocheting through her head. She had been saved by the man of her dreams. The man she trusted with her heart. Her fear was gone. His hands caressed her back, her hair, and finally her face. He squinted at her neck.

"You're bleeding."

"It doesn't matter."

His eyes, his wonderful eyes, gazed deep into her soul.

"It matters to me, babe."

And finally, finally, she believed him.

Adam ran up to them. "Did I get him?"

Jake was on the ground beside Max, checking for a pulse. "He's dead."

Adam dropped the rifle. "I didn't mean to kill him." Adam's voice trembled. "I only wanted to keep him from hurting Grace. I didn't mean to kill anybody."

"You didn't kill him," Jake said. "Your shot went into

his thigh. Mine killed him."

"Thank you. I owe you one," Tyler said.

Grace hugged Adam and then Jake. "Thank you both."

"I was afraid to shoot," Adam said. "But I had to. I couldn't let him kill you, Grace."

"You were very brave, Adam."

Jake clapped Adam on the shoulder. "I owe you, man. When you wounded him, it gave me a clear target."

"So, it's finished," Tyler said.

Chapter Fifteen

Grace woke with a start. She lay quietly listening for the sound that had startled her from sleep. Sometimes she found it hard to believe that she no longer had to fear anything. Her life had turned around. Her whole world had changed.

Tyler left with Jake after shutting down the clinic for an indefinite time. He told her he would be in touch, but she hadn't heard a word in two weeks. Though she tried to deny it, her hopes had died. She'd given her heart to Tyler, believed they would have a future, and set herself up for the pain of losing once again. The blame lay with her and no one else. In time she'd heal, but she'd never forget. Never.

From the foot of the bed Tiffany raised her head and looked at Grace. Sometimes she thought the dog could read her mind.

In the distance, she once again heard the noise that had awakened her. A hammer. Or several hammers. Was someone working on Brad's house?

He'd been released from the hospital, but Harri insisted on keeping him at her place until the cast came off his leg. Grace expected Harri would use the time to make Brad realize how much he needed her.

Grace swung her feet to the floor. "Come on, Tiff. Let's see what's going on."

Tiffany jumped to the floor, stretched her legs and yawned. At least Tyler hadn't lied about his veterinarian skills. Grace dressed without giving a thought to how she looked, for what difference did it make if she looked her best? There was no one who cared.

The pounding of hammers grew louder as Grace

approached Brad's. When she arrived, she couldn't hold back a smile. Adam and several other men were rebuilding the damaged part of the house.

Adam waved and climbed down the ladder. "What do you think?" he asked when he was within shouting distance.

"It's great." She clapped like a child receiving a long-awaited gift.

Adam pulled his cap a little further down to hide his eyes. Grace knew the gesture hid his embarrassment, rather than having a sinister meaning.

"It's the least I can do," he said. "Brad's my best friend."

"Mine, too," she said. "Can I help?"

Adam petted Tiffany, who lately had started accompanying him on his daily walks. They seemed to have become close pals.

"We gotta finish putting up the walls and shingling the roof. But you can help with painting if you like. We should be ready for that by tomorrow."

Grace raised her eyebrows in surprise. "That soon?"

He nodded. "Not that much to do. Mostly the back porch. But the kitchen will need to be cleaned and painted."

"I can handle that," she answered. Her voice trailed off as her attention focused on a familiar figure on the roof.

Adam turned to follow her gaze. "Ain't it great? Tyler's back. Nice of him to help out," he said.

Tyler had returned, but he hadn't called her? Her heart sank. But why should he? She wasn't the type of woman he'd want to spend the rest of his life with, and if he planned on her working at the clinic, he would have called when he returned.

As if sensing her presence, Tyler turned to face her. They were suspended in a moment of time, unanswered questions hanging in the distance separating them.

She tore her gaze away and lifted her lips in a forced

smile. "Adam, I've got some things to take care of, but I'll call you later."

"Okay. I better get back to work." He gave her a shy smile.

"See you later."

"See ya, Grace."

He climbed the ladder and Grace turned to leave. She avoided looking at Tyler, though her heart fluttered frantically against her ribs. She had to get away before the tears unleashed. This time she *would* cry.

She hurried home with Tiffany running ahead as usual. Once there, she grabbed her purse and keys. She had to see Brad. Staying here and worrying about things she had no control over would only lead to misery. She'd had enough of that in the past few weeks to last the rest of her life. She couldn't bear having him so close and knowing he didn't want her, and she couldn't go back to being just friends. Tiffany butted against her leg and whimpered.

Grace ran from the house and started the car. Tears began to flow and she wiped her eyes repeatedly before she could drive. She'd always been a strong person. She could survive this. She always survived. Somehow she'd find a way to forget the feelings Tyler had unleashed in her traitorous body. It was lust, nothing more. Time would fade the memories.

She arrived at Harri's and sat in the car for a moment until she regained control of her raging emotions. Turning the rearview mirror down, she dabbed at the corners of her eyes where dampness still pooled. Could she hide her tears from her friends? She took a deep breath and held it to the count of five, then released. She repeated for several minutes until she lost the urge to cry. Lifting her chin, she walked toward the house.

Brad and Harri seemed glad to see her, and if they noticed she'd been crying, neither acknowledged it. Harri invited her to stay for lunch, then pulled her aside for a private chat, leaving Brad in the kitchen with his ice cream maker.

"What's wrong?" Harri asked. She pointed for Grace to sit in the chair, while Harri chose the bed.

Her bedroom looked just like Harri—a wild splash of colors. Grace glanced at the clothes on the floor. One of Brad's shirts lay there, along with one of Harri's. Muted blue next to vibrant yellow. Grace noticed a pair of men's shoes sticking out from under the bed. Looked like Harri had finally caught her man. That would account for Brad's loud off-key singing competing with the noise from the ice cream machine.

"Nothing's wrong," Grace answered. She met Harri's gaze, her lips lifting in a teasing grin.

"It's not what it looks like," Harri assured her. "Brad asked me to marry him. He's an honorable man. We don't like being apart for long periods of time. At our age, we have to think about things like that."

Brad and Harri...getting married? Grace felt happiness seep into her heart. "Did you say yes?"

Harri's eyes twinkled. "Brad wanted to tell you first before we announced it."

"I won't give away the secret." Grace hugged Harri tight. "Congratulations."

Harri pushed her gently away. "Now tell me what's bothering you. You never cry."

"Tyler's back."

Harri clapped her hands together. "But that's great news, isn't it? Why are you upset?"

"I wouldn't even know he was back if I hadn't seen him working on Brad's roof this morning." Grace bit her bottom lip. "Uh-oh. I guess I'm not so good at keeping a secret after all."

Harri leaned over and patted Grace's knee. "Honey, that's not a secret. Adam told Brad about it a few days ago. Brad's just upset that he can't climb a ladder and help."

"Things will change when I get this blasted cast off," Brad said.

Grace turned to see him leaning on a crutch in the open doorway. How long had he been standing there?

"Adam's a good man," he continued. "Did you know that he and Lainey are getting married next month?" Brad's glance shifted to Harri. His face took on a softer appearance as their eyes met.

"Yes. They invited me to the wedding," Grace said. "Adam's a different man since his picture made the newspaper. He smiles a lot now, too."

"So do I," Brad said, "since I asked Harri to marry me."

"That's wonderful." Grace tried to put surprise in her voice. "I'm so happy for both of you." She forced a smile. "What took you so long?"

"Maybe it took facing death to realize how short life really is. I didn't want to waste any of the rest of the days the good Lord gives me."

Harri patted the mattress beside her. "Come over here and sit down. You shouldn't be standing so long."

Brad grinned. "See what I've got to put up with?"

Grace laughed. "I love you both so much." She hugged Brad, taking the crutch and helping him to the bed.

"There's someone waiting in the kitchen who wants to talk to you," Brad said. He plopped beside Harri, wrapping an arm around her shoulder.

"Me?" Who could be looking for her? Unless—

Her pulse quickened. A soft woof brought a smile to her face. She'd recognize Tiffany's bark anywhere.

"Go on," Brad said. "Don't keep the young man waiting."

Grace made her way to the kitchen on trembling legs. Her breath caught in her throat when she saw Tyler. His eyes were that same shade of green, deep, dark and mysterious.

****

Tyler patted his pocket to make sure he hadn't forgotten the package. "Hi, Grace," he said.

"You didn't call."

"I'm sorry. I didn't get here until late last night. I wanted to surprise you, but your lights were off." God she was even more beautiful than he remembered. Her hair curled softly around her face and he wanted to crush her in his arms. "Adam left a message asking if I would lend a hand repairing Brad's house. I stopped by your place on the way this morning, but you were still sleeping. I didn't want to disturb you."

"Are...are you back to stay then?"

He took a step toward her. "Absolutely. I turned in my gun and gave Jake my notice. I would have been back sooner, but I spent a few days with my dad. He's going to move here and work in the clinic with us..."

"Us?"

He closed the gap between them and circled his arms around her waist. "Yes, us. Dad can't wait to meet you."

"Me?" Her voice squeaked out.

Tyler nodded. "I told him all about you. How brave you are, how beautiful you are, and how stubborn you are." He watched the emotions chasing across her face. She started to protest, but Tyler stopped her with a warm, consuming kiss. She clung to him and he knew then that he'd finally come home. Tyler broke the kiss and smiled down at her. He lifted her off her feet and kissed her again. Their eyes were now on an even level.

He touched his nose to hers. "I love you, Grace Wilkins."

"I love you back."

Tyler eased her feet to the floor and reached one arm out to open the screen door.

Tiffany raced into the room wriggling between them. Tyler rested a hand on the dog's nose. "I wanted the two of you to be together for this." He looked deeply into Grace's blue eyes, now dark as the bluest seas. He took the ring from his pocket and knelt on the floor. He took Grace's hand.

"I've already gotten permission from Brad." He

smiled. "Grace, will you and Tiffany marry me?"

"Yes," she answered.

Tiffany barked her acceptance.

And Tyler knew he'd found the peace he sought in the love shining from Grace's eyes.

About the author...

Carol resides in Columbus, Ohio, and supports her writing career by working as an Executive Administrative Assistant. Her bookshelves overflow with novels written by her favorite authors. Give her a good mystery, a bit of nail-biting, and a satisfying love story and she's content to while away the hours. Even more than reading romantic suspense novels, she loves to write them.

She's a member of Romance Writers of America, RWA Kiss of Death Chapter, and Pop Fiction Writers. She credits her friends in Pop Fiction with keeping her motivated and inspired to continue writing.